C000294858

The Star

An Amanda Buckingham Brief Case

and

The Courageous Witness

by

Oliver Richbell

Published by City Fiction

Copyright © 2019 2020 Oliver Richbell

The right of Oliver Richbell to be identified as the author of this work has been asserted by him in accordance with the Copyright, Designs and Patents Act 1988

ISBN: 978-1-910040-38-6

SEASON 1: CASE 2
THE STAR WITNESS

He never saw the punch coming until it was too late.

The two pugilists resembled a pair of drunken teenagers on the dance floor as they grappled and held each other in a sweaty hazy embrace. The boxers were three and a half rounds into a most uninspiring boxing bout that was so far down on the card of scheduled fights that the TV cameras on each corner of the ring were not even switched on.

A smaller than sparse crowd were paying little or no attention; the occasional glance up from their mobile phones seemed sufficient for them to verify that the fighters were still entwined together like the wires to a set of headphones found in the depths of a sports bag.

One of the few spectators had looked up just three times from his hand held screen and this was only as a result of hearing the bell that was clearly audible in the all but vacant O2 Arena situated on the Greenwich peninsular in South East London. This Pavlovian response had resulted in seeing nothing of the actual fight itself but instead merely viewing the two men returning to their respective corners.

The uppercut came from nowhere.

It was a devastating blow aided, in no small way, by it being thrown at the perfect time as both men finally staggered apart.

The sound of bone crumbling is not pleasant, and it takes a hardened soul to move in for the kill. There was no hesitation here though as one of the gladiatorial warriors stepped purposefully forward with a powerful clenched fist.

1

The guttural noises that echoed from the four cornered boxing ring had caused those in attendance, for a few brief moments at least, to lose interest in their handsets. The assembled collection of random observers recoiled in horror as they pulled the goldfish facial expression that one tends to adopt when witnessing an impending car accident and being entirely unable to do anything to stop it.

However, the intended punch never landed. There was no need for it. The fight was over. If truth be told it was the archetypical mismatch anyway - an undefeated young up-and-comer against a journeyman who had lost far more bouts than he had won.

The referee bravely stepped in and straight into the path of the impending blow with his arms waving frantically like he was being attacked by a swarm of wasps and he declared that the fight was over. One man stood victorious; the other now laid sprawled on the canvas staring vacantly at the thousands of spotlights above.

***

It was a minute or two before six fifteen on a mild Saturday evening in central London and Amanda Buckingham was looking forward to a hot bath and an early night. Her pink-flowered cheongsam was loosely tied around her midriff and Rumpole, her cantankerous cat who had put plenty of weight back on after recent surgery, lay across her legs fast asleep. Amanda was feeling comfortably content although slightly fuzzy-headed after a lunch with Trevor Hamper-Houghton, a colleague from her barrister's chambers.

The food itself was pleasant enough, a super food salad that consisted of quinoa, sweet potatoes, fresh peas, broccoli and chilli flakes, however it was not really sufficient for the two glasses of white wine Amanda drank alongside. It was actually three glasses as she had not finished her second and had merely topped herself up. The company was adequate, it passed the time and it was a most welcome distraction after the chaotic week she had undergone.

Amanda had not lost a case in her legal career to date and she was the rising star at Hartington Chambers, although she never publicly flouted her perfect record. Trevor, on the other hand, was a decent barrister who had a gift for advising in writing on legal merit, but he lacked the advocacy skill and the art of thinking quickly on his feet that the better barristers possessed. Amanda, however, had it all; a ferocious intelligence coupled with the human touch that made her approachable and respected by her clients, the judiciary, her peers and most importantly the members of the public that would make up the juries.

Her week had been difficult to say the least. It had started with the usual Monday morning deluge of questions from the administration team at Hartington Chambers. Dave Blyth, the senior clerk, wanted to know exactly what she had planned for the week ahead.

"Miss," he always used the deferential title when addressing her, "I have a number of updates for you". At the time Amanda was standing next to Trevor in the clerk's room and, in an attempt to show eagerness, he jumped into a conversation that he was not involved in with, "anything for me, David?"

Dave had always been a Dave even since he was a child at a south London comprehensive – his business card and even email used Dave and yet for some inexplicable reason some members of Chambers like Trevor Hamper-Houghton and its Head, Rufus Hetherington-Jones QC, would only refer to him as David. It pissed Dave off a lot and he often wondered whether it was just a peculiarity associated with posh twats with hyphens in their names or whether it was a natural consequence of privilege. He always settled on the former explanation as he was proud of his working class background and despite the fact that he was now rubbing shoulders with some of society's elite he would often joke that the nearest thing he ever got to privy-ledge as a child was the window sill in the toilet.

So with a quiet brutality that would have shaken the most hardened of souls Dave glanced to his left to an empty corner of the long mahogany table that supported the hefty weight of neatly bundled papers then he slowly brought his eyes in line with Trevor's. "Nothing as of yet," he replied and after a second or so of piercing silence he muttered an almost inaudible, "Sir".

Amanda spent her week flying from meetings, to Court and back to Chambers. Trevor spent his time preparing a precise itinerary for his upcoming trip to Bilbao.

***

Sat on his stool in the sparsely populated venue in south London, Ricky O'Ryan had won again. He remained undefeated with now a perfect record of six fights, six wins and all by knockout.

He was breathing hard as the adrenaline that coursed through his veins was now wearing off. His trainer and manager, a wily veteran by the name of Stephen Robertson, was reliving the knockout in ever increasing grandiose terms. "What a punch," he was screaming, "What a great shot! Wow Ricky unbelievable; where on earth did that come from?"

Ricky heard the question but failed to answer as he was peering over Robertson's left shoulder watching his opponent receive medical treatment. Kris 'The Sleep Maker' Baker was a mess. His legs were kicking like a baby, but his arms were prostrate to each side of his head. The Grant 10oz boxing gloves were still firmly on his hands.

The British Boxing Board of Control officials and the ring announcer were ready to enlighten a practically empty auditorium of the winner of the fight so Stephen helped Ricky to his feet as they made their way to the centre of the ring. Baker didn't move or even attempt to.

"The Referee calling an end to the contest at one minute forty-eight seconds of the third round and the winner, by technical knockdown, and still undefeated... Ricky 'Star Man' O'Ryan".

No-one cheered or even seemed to care; there might have been a further smattering of applause, but it was much more likely to have been the ratter-tat-tat of seats being snapped closed as the spectators headed for the bar or food stalls in the bowels of the O2 Arena.

Ricky pulled on his robe. It was jet black with silver trim and on the back, it sparkled with the words; Ricky 'Star Man' O'Ryan and across the shoulders was a perfect portrayal of 'Orion's Belt'. It was his Mother who, from their home in Northern Ireland, had first called him her 'Star Man' and not least because he had four sisters. As soon as he took up the noble art of pugilism she had created the image of Orion's Belt and even before he had turned professional Ricky had promised her that one day he would be a world champion and bring his own O'Ryan's Belt back for her and the rest of the family.

In the ring there was no congratulatory hug from the promoter or interviews with the media or high fives from proud sponsors – it was a solitary arm aloft and then off and away towards the changing rooms.

As Stephen and Ricky walked past bank after bank of empty seats he stopped and took one last look towards the stage. Kris 'The Sleep Maker' Baker was thankfully now upright and moving slowly. He was being supported by his team as they carefully guided him down from the ring. Kris' career had never lived up to the early promise of a fine amateur record and his boxing nickname, that he himself had chosen, had never been prophetically successful; unless he had planned to put the crowd to sleep. Kris didn't know it at the time, but he'd never fight professionally again.

Back in his tiny dressing room Ricky messaged his Mum "I won. Love you xx". Stephen was on his phone calling the local Northern Irish media in the vain hope that they'd run a short story in the paper or online about their latest victory. Ricky sat hunched on the wooden slatted bench thinking about going out for some beers with a couple of his friends who had made the trip over to see him fight. They'd not actually seen him though as they were enjoying some minor backstage hospitality of warm bottled lager and a couple of bowls of mixed nuts.

Ricky was heading for a well-earned shower when his phone buzzed. "So proud of you my Star Man. One more step towards O'Ryan's Belt! Love Mum c". His phone whirred again, his Mum had corrected the common text error and sent a further message simply "Xxx".

He headed for the shower and was looking forward to a night out. He'd been 'in camp' for a little over eight weeks and he was ready to let off a lot of steam and hopefully 'get some'. Ricky had not had sex for nearly three months and standing under the tepid water jets he felt the urge for some casual, no strings adult fun.

***

Amanda hadn't moved and neither had Rumpole. Her phone vibrated somewhere on the sofa where they both lay. It was Trevor. "I have managed to acquire two tickets to the boxing event this evening that we discussed earlier over lunch. Would you be interested in attending with me?"

Amanda smiled at the overt lack of any 'text speak' from him but he was certainly sending her mixed messages, one day it was 'you're not my type' the next was let's go for lunch and now he was suggesting an evening out. She didn't reply straightaway as she had no interest in watching boxing, but she did enjoy the workout side of the sport with Zach, her personal trainer, who encouraged her to do it for the cardio benefits. She also relished the physicality and she'd often undertake some pad work in the run up to a trial as she found it was the perfect way for her to release the pent-up aggression that she always felt before a big case...

Amanda sat with her phone in one hand as she rubbed Rumpole's contented stomach with the other. After a few idle attempts at a witty reply the response sent was as formal as the message received; "Sorry Trevor I'm back home and have a sofa date with Rumpole. Enjoy the boxing. A".

Trevor went to the boxing with a chap he had become friendly with from his local tennis club. He didn't enjoy his evening. He was not certain how many bouts he sat through, but he spent most of the time drafting a series of further messages to Amanda, but he never sent any of them.

***

Ricky was dressed in a faux pair of Converse trainers, ripped jeans and a tight white T-shirt with an image of the 1970's rock band 'The Ramones' across its crumpled front. There was no 24-hour porterage or laundry service at his hotel and even though he was a professional boxer with a perfect record he was put up in a budget chain of hotels the other side of the river towards London's West End. He just had to put up with it for now. The 'top of the bill' fighters and their entire gargantuan entourage were replete with the surroundings of five star luxury suites and rooms and Ricky had wistfully looked at the warming yellow luminosity of the lights of the ornate and grand entrance to these superior hotels which they passed in the back of the black cab as they approached the O2 Arena a few hours earlier. Ricky had turned to Stephen and asked, "Do you think we'll ever get to stay in that type of hotel?" Stephen, ever the diplomat, responded with genuine paternal affection. "If you keep winning son then you'll be sponsored by them one day".

Standing with his sports bag slung over his left shoulder Ricky was ready to get out of the belly of the beast. The venue's Operations Director, a greasy weaselly rotund person whose name neither Stephen, Ricky nor anyone else ever bothered to remember was ushering them both out of the restricted area as if they were the last two in a pub at closing time.

Stephen was hopeful of a quick word with the show's main promoter, Ethan Harris of SportsSpace Boxing. They went way back, or so Stephen would claim, and he was desperate to stake a claim for Ricky's next fight and onward progression up the ranks until hopefully he would get a shot at a title and a world champion's belt.

Ethan was not to be found though, at least not in person, but his image was on display in Ultra HD, on the myriad of television screens that seemed to be mounted on every wall. There was no volume, but subtitles were on and although the lip-sync was out Ethan was being interviewed by Adam Smith of Sky Boxing alongside Dave Coldwell and Carl Froch. Ethan was 'bigging up' the main event of the evening as two contenders were going to fight it out for the chance to become the World Boxing Association's mandatory heavyweight challenger. Dave Coldwell, who, as a world-class trainer, had masterminded some of British boxing's greatest nights, nodded his agreement. Carl Froch, a former multiple World Champion boxer excitedly jumped into state that this was a massive night for the heavyweight boxing division. Adam Smith stood motionless, saying nothing, but was evidently delighted with the way three icons of the sport were promoting the impending main attraction.

Stephen brushed off his disappointment with a quick glance back to Ricky, "I'll call him next week," as he flicked his head towards the latest flat screen TV as they passed. Ricky smiled back although he didn't really feel like doing so as he trudged behind Stephen. As they both walked slowly back into the main holding area Ricky checked his phone. 'No Service' and as he roughly forced his large mobile back into the tight pocket of his skinny ripped denim trousers he heard, "Hey mate".

Ricky's eyes shot up with a twinkle that those with Irish blood were so fortunate to enjoy. He was hopeful that this audible introduction was going to be a precursor to a deeper conversation about his earlier triumphant win.

The "Hey mate" had come from a Sky Sports technician dressed in a yellow hi vis jacket that was at least three sizes too big and he also sported the largest set of headphones Ricky had ever seen. As they approached each other down the narrow passageway inside the arena they passed without even the hint of a halt in either's gait and as they did so the engineer stuck up a pale bony fist in a thumbs up gesture and declared, "Great T-Shirt". There was no other acknowledgement, no well done, no request for an autograph and to be fair Ricky doubted that the man had even recognised him as one of the fighters given that his bout was not even being shown on Sky Sports television.

Finally, after a walk that lasted longer than his earlier fight, Ricky found himself back in the cordoned off holding zone. Stephen had paced ahead a few moments earlier and was deeply engrossed already with a group of suited men; their lanyards clearly showed "P" for Press and Stephen, as ever, was doing his utmost to try and get 'The Star Man' a little bit of media sparkle. It didn't work, but at least he was trying his best thought Ricky.

Ricky saw his two friends lecherously poring over a couple of women who appeared to be doing anything they could not to sit still long enough for a male arm to be draped over their shoulders. He approached them with little interest in joining their sport but with Stephen trying to engage with the reporters in the vain hope that his energetically theatrical replay of the knockout blow would encourage them to at least add a by-line to their write up of the headline bout, there was no-one else to talk to or even approach. Ricky's kitbag dangled by its lengthy strap over his head and left shoulder, so it hung and bounced against his right thigh. He resembled, as he walked, a 'Han Solo' cowboyesque character but instead of a low-belted blaster he sported a battered old bag full of sweaty wet and dirty clothes.

His two friends, Connor and Michael, saw him approach and they greeted him with the utter adulation that only drunk men can offer. "Here he is" and the three exchanged meaningful man-hugs. Ricky was not offered a drink or even asked how he was as Connor and Michael turned back to their prey and with supercilious tones announced, "See I told you 'The Star Man' was our mate". Ricky, not for the first or last time that evening, smiled meekly.

"Drop your fuckin' bag and join us for a drink!" slurred Michael.

"Yeah," followed up Connor, "get the beers in too," and with the predatorial advances of a stalking fox he added, "and a couple of whatever the fuck these two are knocking back."

One of the women, a twenty-two-year-old

postgraduate in social media studies by the name of Becka, quipped, "So Connor tell us my friend's name and we will stay for another drink". She made it absolutely clear that she pronounced his forename carefully and loudly enough for all of their little gathering to overhear

Michael roared with laughter and pointed mockingly to his friend with his right hand as he dragged his left arm over Becka's shoulders, so his hand fell 'accidentally' over the top of her chest. Liz, their other quarry, was a bright, sassy woman of twenty-two years who had just completed a midwifery course at Hertfordshire University. She sat there with her best poker face on as Connor clearly had not paid any attention to anything they had said.

All eyes were on Connor and this was the 'make or break' moment which despite the obvious nature of her next comment was expertly delivered. Perched on the high stools that encompassed the pop-up circular bar tables she calmly added, "But don't tell him your name though Abi …". Connor took the bait as all boys would have done in that situation. "Come on Abi, of course I knew that! So, what can we get you to drink?" Ricky was entirely aware that the "we" referred solely to him.

With ice-cold ruthlessness the girls, like they were synchronised swimmers, slipped off the stools and just at the moment their high heeled shoes landed on the hard tiled floor Liz looked straight into Connor's eyes and said with an ice-cold delivery, "My name is not Abi".

Liz and Becka sauntered away arm-in-arm giggling at how stupid some 'boys' can be. Two of the three men were left to argue amongst themselves who had 'fucked up a sure thing'. Connor and Michael exchanged their wildly biased opinions on who was to blame but Ricky watched the two women casually stroll away with an internal comment of 'fair play both'.

Stephen joined the demi-throng grasping two bottles of tepid continental lager in each hand. Ricky was grateful for the interruption. As he took a well-earned swig of beer, he left his two friends to their seemingly unending 'blame game' and asked of Stephen, "So anything?" Those two words were not intended to be so cutting but the recipient recoiled slightly and took solace in his bottle as he mentally fumbled for a reply, "You never know do you …? They seemed interested and I told them all about your wonder punch in the third round …", and in a deflection move that most politicians would have been proud of Stephen answered the question asked of him with an enquiry of his own, "You've still not told me where it came from by the way".

Ricky smiled back, "It was a stellar shot from The Star Man". Stephen let out a head back roar of laughter and chinked his bottle with Ricky's and they both took another long swig of its contents.

The reception area began to empty as another undercard bout was about to begin; this one included a local Londoner fighting in the cruiserweight division.

Ricky had no interest in this fight, or any of the other build-up bouts or even the Main Event of the night so he took off his yellow lanyard and photo I.D. tag that identified him as a competitor which would have enabled him access to a special but secluded area to watch the fights. He wound the coloured ribbon around the plastic-coated tag and stuffed it into his left trouser pocket.

The four beers didn't last long not least because Connor managed to spill most of his over the table as he was trying to gesticulate his innocence in why the two women had left. Ricky walked towards the hatch-bar in order to replenish their refreshments in the hope that respite for his downcast state could be found in booze. He caught the attention of the barman and tried to raise a smile to inject a degree of connection before he got served. The savage reply was a shake of the head as the shutters were pulled down before his very eyes. Instead of a round of drinks Ricky came face-to-face with a printed sign that read "No Service during bouts by order of SportsSpace Boxing". As he turned back, he roughly yanked his phone out of his pocket "No Service" said the screen.

"Let's get outta here and find a proper boozer", asserted Ricky. Connor and Michael immediately forgot their disagreement and yawped their collective agreement. Stephen nodded his.

As the four men exited the venue the noise from the amphitheatre rose to a crescendo with the crowd baying for violence as if they were all back seated in the Roman Colosseum watching gladiators kill for their collective amusement.

A string of black cabs were tightly queued up outside resembling a child's string toy and, jumping into the first hackney carriage, the four men all tried desperately not to be stuck on the two fold down seats that face the wrong way of travel. Stephen and Connor soon swapped as the latter declared "I'll spew my guts up if I sit backwards". Ricky's holdall was in the middle of the back seat next to him and opposite was a drunken and cross looking Michael.

Stephen gave the hotel's address and they sped off

into the crisp London night and away from the glittering O2 Arena.

"What's up with your face?" said Ricky.

"Nothing … They were fuckin' slags anyway, mate".

"Slags?", thought Ricky, "so why are they not coming back to the hotel with us then?"

"Mate, they were fuckin' prick teasers".

"And we've probably had a lucky escape as I don't fancy a trip to the clinic in the morning". Connor roared with laughter and waggled his thumb and little finger in salute of the apparently hilarious proclamation.

Ricky sat there in utter disbelief and wondered how and why he was still hanging out with such moronic creatures. The three of them had been friends for years having grown up on the unforgiving streets of Belfast. Technically they'd all been in the same class at school, but education was not what they went to school for. More was learnt about life and how to get by on the concrete outside the school gates than in its classrooms. All three began boxing at a tender age but Ricky was the talent. Connor and Michael occasionally used to refer to him as 'Jack' because in a scrap there was no one that he could not fell like a lumberjack working in a forest. It also amused them that Jack O'Ryan could be the Irish version of the hero from a few of Tom Clancy's novels, not that they'd ever read one in their lives, but they'd watched all the movies.

Despite the need for men to try and impress upon their peers that they are 'bad men', none of the three got into any real trouble, except with the truant officer. They joined their local boxing gym more out of a sense of 'why not' than anything else and two of them fought bravely but without skill at junior amateur level. Ricky was talent-spotted as a star of the future from his early teenage years. It was Stephen who developed and honed the natural flair for fighting into an accomplished craft and ultimately into a career. Ricky's love and respect for Stephen was unfettered but as he rested his now weary legs in the back of the black cab, he struggled to rationalise how Connor and Michael were making his life better. He recalled some sage words from his Father; "Son, there are makers and takers in this world. Don't waste your time with takers". It was not that prophetically insightful but for Ricky they were words he would never forget.

As the taxi wound its way through the capital's nightlife the pointless chatter was interrupted by the cabbie, "So lads you didn't fancy the fight then?".

"What's that mate?", replied Stephen

"The boxing", bellowed back the driver, "You didn't fancy watching it?" As with most of his profession he was ready to tell you his viewpoint as was, of course, sacrosanct, "It's all fixed anyway, it's no better than those Yanks that pretend to wrestle".

Ricky and Stephen exchanged quizzical looks as if they were both saying, "who asked him?"

The silence was taken as a tacit acceptance for the continuation of the monologue. "Yeah, you know what I'm saying don't you...... it's all a con. Those promoters just give a few quid out to fix the fight and people like you and me get it the hard way".

Nothing came back from the back of his cab, so he pressed on: "It's not like it used to be back in the day is it now?" Whilst it might have sounded like a question it must have been a rhetorical one as there was no pause for an answer, not that any of his passengers were willing to give one. "Yeah, you know what I mean - the classic fights Bruno v Benn and the other black fella with the lorry who fought the other one".

With such "knowledge" what could the professional boxer respond with? The fact it was actually Eubank v Benn as Bruno was a heavyweight and could never have fought Benn at middleweight level was irrelevant. It was just the typical rant of the ill-informed. Ricky didn't rise but Stephen did. "Do you not mean Chris Eubank, who had a truck, who actually fought Nigel Benn in 1990 and 1993?"

"That's what I mean right, it's not as good as it used to be and the modern rematches are always rubbish", said the cabbie.

"What about the Froch Groves, Haye Bellew, Chisora Whyte fights to name but a few," retaliated Stephen.

"Here we are then chaps," was the only reply as the cab pulled up outside the modest entrance at their unexceptional destination. The exorbitant fee was paid together with a minimal tip and the four men disembarked their carriage with mutterings of gratitude.

"Enjoy your night anyway lads, looks like you've got a nice place....". And with that their erstwhile carriage sped away with its lights cutting into the blackness ahead.

"Five-minute turnaround boys then back out", was the order from Ricky.

Four minutes later after Ricky had dropped off his bag and he had applied some product to his hair and Connor and Michael had taken a bath in cheap eau-de-cologne, the three were stood in what could only be loosely described as the lobby of the hotel. They were all smartly dressed but with the amount of denim on show they could have been mistaken for the male equivalent of the Irish girl band B*Witched.

A minute later Stephen appeared checking his watch as he walked. He was not late, but his fashion sense most definitely was.

"What the fuckin' hell do you look like?", cried Michael.

Stephen was wearing cherry red chino trousers, brilliant white pumps and a neon-blue Hawaiian shirt with even more garish pineapples spewed all over it.

"What's wrong with it?", asked Stephen as he looked down to check himself over.

"Sorry mate I can't hear you over that shirt", sniggered Connor.

The four men returned to London's streets and headed the short distance towards the Covent Garden Piazza, stopping at each and every pub along the way.

***

Amanda had fallen asleep.

The 'two' glasses of wine at lunch time had caught up with her and despite the best intentions of cleaning her Clerkenwell flat, or at the very least tidying away some of life's clutter, she was focused on bed. An idea came into her head that perhaps some company would be nice, but actually she was now too tired to be bothered.

Rumpole sauntered towards his bowl only to be disappointed at the paucity of its contents. He turned and meowed the cry of a cat that had never been fed before. Temperance and patience are not characteristics that this particular cat possessed. A further, and more desperate sounding plea for sustenance was emitted.

"Okay okay, Rumpy I heard you the first time". The look that Rumpole gave to his owner in response could only be described as 'well if you heard me the first time then why I am not eating already?'.

Amanda ripped open a packet of wet cat food but despite this being a particular brand of luxury beef chunks in gravy, it is nigh on impossible to tear the opening off in one clean motion. Amanda, tired and more than a little in the pre-hungover stage went for the flap and squeeze approach straight into Rumpole's dish. The problem with this approach is that you need a third hand with which to fend off the waiting mouth whilst at the same time holding back the dangling plastic strip in an attempt to force the food out of the limited opening. Amanda washed her hands in the kitchen sink and was so desperate for bed that she headed towards her bedroom wiping her wet hands on the sides of her now open cheongsam.

Amanda fell into a deep sleep almost as her head hit her crisp white linen covered pillow. Other than the occasional stretch from Rumpole, who had taken up his usual position in the centre of the bed, both occupants barely moved until morning and the cat decided he was hungry again.

***

There was no such tranquillity for Stephen, Connor, Michael or Ricky. Their late evening had begun so promisingly with a few quid in their collective pockets and plenty of alcohol in their bloodstream but as often is the case with 'boys and beer' it ended in the stereotypical brawl.

One of the four had already been in an earlier fight but that one at least had guidelines – "The Queensbury Rules" which dated all the way back to 1867. The noble art had changed a great deal since those halcyon days and one thing was for certain, the fight that 'kicked off' in London's West End actually had more onlookers to it than Ricky's earlier professional bout.

Ricky, sleep deprived, hung-over and in a foul temper departed Charing Cross Police Station. Sat on the steps of the building opposite were Stephen, Michael and Connor all looking and smelling terrible as they had all stayed outside on the streets all night waiting for Ricky to reappear. There was no conversation as they trudged towards the hotel and their immaculately pressed beds.

***

Amanda's Sunday started like most other days. Rumpole strode across her prone stomach and as usual that paunchy cat was able to find the perfect spot to pressurise the bladder. Amanda swore in her native Cantonese: "*Diu*," she cried as she sat bolt upright. She'd been dozing for twenty minutes or so enjoying her large comfy bed, it was from 'Loaf' the upmarket furniture supplier and had cost her a small fortune but she loved it, and as with most things Amanda purchased, as long as she could rationalise the usage against the price tag it was fine. She really didn't need to worry about money at all though having already been very well provided for by the trust funds set up by her Father although she didn't tend to splurge or treat herself with too many extravagances.

Now awake and needing the toilet Amanda ruffled Rumpole's fur and swinging her legs out of the bed with a martial arts style kick she was up and heading for the bathroom. Rumpole moved with the speed of a hare around a dog track to be under her manicured feet almost causing Amanda to trip over him. "Diu" exclaimed Amanda again but staring down at the love of her life she realised that a few moments peace was impossible when Rumpole wanted food.

***

As the four bedraggled men snaked through London's backstreets it was not long before Michael chirped up, "Could 'av been fuckin' avoided if dickhead over there could remember some tart's name," – he pointed to Connor as he spoke and he had hoped that this faux rapier-like wit would help bring the gang back together. It didn't.

Stephen shook his head as he plodded onwards.

Connor scowled back and responded eruditely with, "Go fuck yourself!"

Ricky didn't even acknowledge this exchange as he was lost deep in his thoughts about the events of the last few hours. Stephen, with a paternal instinct, eased his gait alongside Ricky's as Michael and Connor continued their petulant repartee behind them; "No you fuck yourself."

"No, you."

"No, YOU!"

"So, what did the Peelers say then Ricky?" as he spoke he draped a protective arm over the shoulder of the young boxer. It was an anachronistic reference to the police force, but Ricky knew his history.

"No charge yet while they continue their enquiries but I'm not to go home and I was told I might have to surrender my passport".

"Fuck," was the almost instantaneous reaction from Stephen.

"Yeah," came back Ricky.

The monosyllabic conversation continued for a few more paces until the two men stepped into a weary and depressing silence. The same cannot be said of the two boys behind them who were now engaged in an apparent competition in seeing who could include the most profanities into their sentences.

Ricky and Stephen were now deeply engrossed in their separate thoughts. Stephen was deliberating how he was going to explain this one to Ethan Harris and the SportsSpace team. He was the boxer's trainer and manager but there was no debate as to who the top dog was. Ethan had been in boxing literally all is life due to his Dad's firm SportsSpace Sports. Billy Harris made his name in sports promoting on the back of the explosion of snooker in the 1980s and as well as darts the noble art of boxing proved to be a major area for Team Harris. Ethan joined the family firm and in just a few short years he had become the U.K.'s number one promoter. Others may have tried to disagree, but longevity is no substitute for ability.

The major problem that Stephen was foreseeing was having to explain to Ethan that 'The Star Man' had spent the evening in a police cell. The immediate risk to Ricky, from Stephen's point of view, was not actually the authorities but the possibility that Ethan terminated the promotional agreement because he didn't want any adverse publicity being brought to SportsSpace's door.

Ricky's thoughts were not so intricate. All he could think about was how, only a fistful of hours earlier, he had been winning another fight and out for beers and a fun-time in London and then he ended up spending the night banged up.

Stephen had made a decision. Back in their hotel room and sat on his bed, a single in a double room that he shared with Ricky, he decided he was not going anywhere and he was going to stick with Ricky and do whatever he could to help. Judging from the racket through the flimsy walls Connor and Michael, who had paid for a twin room themselves along with their flights over from Belfast, were hastily getting ready to bolt.

Ricky came out of the bathroom and leant against the partition wall and for the first time in what seemed like an age he began a conversation with Stephen.

"What am I going to do?", Stephen picked up on the individuality of the statement straightaway and replied.

"What we are going to do is call Ethan and tell him everything." Stephen stressed the 'we' as he spoke, and it gained a flicker of a smile from Ryan.

After a pause that was far shorter than it felt he continued.

"First of all, Ricky I think I need to know everything."

***

Amanda's Sunday was spent as they often were, in the gym and her home office. Her workout was good although she felt a little more self-conscious than usual as her preferred exercise bike was being brutalised by a portly chap trying to defy the laws of ageing. Amanda was left to hop on the only remaining bike that was inappropriately placed near the water-dispenser in a way that meant when those needing to quench their thirst and they put their mouth to the tap the natural angle of their head stared straight towards Amanda's bottom as it wiggled to her cycling rhythm. Normally she quite liked her bum but there was no need to literally thrust it into people's faces.

After an uninspiring lunch of a shop bought Cajun chicken wholemeal wrap her mind naturally, like so many barristers and legal professionals, turned to the forthcoming week's case load. Her Clerkenwell flat was perfectly laid out for her chosen career. Her 'chosen career' had quite a lot of legal interpretation applied to it given that it was her father, Arthur Buckingham, who had chosen her career.

Amanda's flat was more than modest and for its area of the capital it was not cheap by any means. Again, not that money was an issue given the trust funds carefully set up by her father. She was mortgage free with a hefty monthly allowance and to some a career as a socialite would have been the stress-free option but that was just not Amanda. Nor indeed was the path followed by some in Amanda's position, a job as a part time lawyer just working on the odd case here and there simply to stop the shopping or travelling becoming overly monotonous.

Amanda was 'all in' as a barrister and this was most evident in her approach to every single case and client. There was so much more to practicing Law than the 'win' or the money. Amanda really believed that it was a vocation and although there were no loving 'in memoriam' photos of her late father around her home due to his libidinous behaviour and descent into alcoholism, she did appreciate what he had provided for her. She had breezed through her law degree at Lady Margaret Hall Oxford, which included a year at the Université Patheon-Assas in Paris and she joined Hartington Chambers, a leading criminal law barrister's set in Lincoln's Inn, straight from Oxford University.

Many years later, with a perfect record of having never lost a case Amanda was not just the rising star at Hartington Chambers but also of the Criminal Bar. She was envied and respected in equal measure, although it was more the former in private and the latter in public, but it was Amanda's approach and style to her clients that truly set her apart. Amanda's tactical brain was so fine-tuned it could win Le Mans 24, but it was her tactile grace that meant her charges trusted her immediately and placed themselves entirely in her capable hands without hesitation or second thought. University and Law School taught her the mechanics of what you need to practice, but her people skills and interpersonal relationship building were never on the curriculum and cannot be learnt from a textbook or webinar. They are ingrained deep within a person's DNA and you either have them or are found wanting. The most successful lawyers do, and Amanda most certainly did.

Her afternoon was spent sat at her Antique French Kingwood Bureau Plat with the late afternoon sun streaming over the London rooftops and onto her papers, while she began her preparations for what looked like yet another busy week. This writing desk was picked up for a 'steal' whilst she an undergraduate in Paris and it was one of her most cherished possessions. The ormolu style of gold leaf and the dark colour of Kingwood made it stand out in

Amanda's modern flat but she could not bear to be away from it and had paid a small fortune to have it transported over from Paris to her Uncle and Aunt's house in St John's Wood and then onto Clerkenwell. As the removal men were carefully carrying it up the stairs to her flat it was commented that it was a 'nice bit of stuff'. For Amanda it embodied the very beginnings of her legal career and it had never let her down as it made her feel invincible when she poured over her laptop or the bundles of legal documents placed upon it.

Amanda's most recent case of note was a successful prosecution of two men charged with sexual assault and rape. The two accused were rightfully found guilty, but Amanda was only too aware that the victim had been so brave in staring down her assailants in giving evidence at the trial. Amanda doubted that she could have done what the victim had been able to do - she really was the courageous witness. For Amanda the outcome was the right one although her legal opponent, a disgusting toad of a man, by the name of Archie Morton, had tried every dirty trick he could think of to persuade the jury that the two men were entirely blameless. In the end justice was done and most importantly was seen to have been done

With her laptop to the right of her Counsel's note pad and her blue ink pen held delicately in her left-hand Amanda was preparing an opinion on a forthcoming conference with a criminal defence solicitors firm, Messrs Smith Steyn. They were not a regular source of work but Hartington Chambers' senior clerk; Dave Blyth reminded her that the occasional instruction, with a good job done, will often always lead to more work for her and Chambers. Amanda didn't react to the oxymoronic use of 'often always' as Dave was not the sort of person to enjoy being picked up on his language by someone half his age. The relationship between clerks and barristers was strained at the best of times as they were from different sides of the track, but Amanda never ever treated them as her underlings; after all they were the front-facing team who worked the relationships with those sending in the paid work for the barristers. This was a lesson that Amanda had learnt from Day One; her colleague and roommate at Chambers, Trevor Hamper-Houghton, was still yet to comprehend the importance of this.

After a few more hours of analytical reasoning Amanda typed up her opinion and filed it away for sending out on Monday morning. Not everyone worked a Sunday afternoon after all, and she didn't want to interrupt anyone with a work email on the weekend that could easily wait until the fast-approaching Monday.

***

Eight calls to Ethan Harris had not been answered. Stephen's call log on his battered iPhone 7 showed there had been eleven minutes from the first unanswered call to the last. Ricky and Stephen had not spoken a word to each other for at least double that amount of time.

The ninth call again rang to voicemail and Stephen pressed the large red circle to cancel the call.

Ricky had been sat on his bed, legs apart and feet on the floor. His elbows were on his thighs and hands on head, it resembled the 'brace position' he'd seen in the inflight safety card on his flight over from Belfast a few days before. It felt like a lifetime ago. He didn't adjust his position and mumbled towards the frayed carpet, "Why don't you leave him a message?" Stephen replied with what he felt was an astute reason, "I'm not sure we want there to be a recording do we?" The 'we' was less emphasised than before, but Ricky nodded his agreement.

There was no need for a tenth call as Stephen's phone began to vibrate and ring. His ringtone chirped away to the tune of David Bowie's "Star Man" which was the same walk-in music that Ricky used for his ring-walk entrance music. The lyrics were seemingly written for Ricky 'The Star Man' O'Ryan:

> *"There's a starman waiting in the sky*
> *He's told us not to blow it*
> *Cause he knows it's all worthwhile"*

Stephen reacted like he was a contestant on a gameshow as the incoming call was answered as if his life depended on it.

"Ethan I am so sorr…" was all he could say before he was interrupted.

"Look, what's so urgent that you've called me a dozen times on a Sunday?" was audibly heard by both men without Stephen even having to turn the speakerphone on. Stephen let the miscalculation go, it was not the time nor the place nor even the person to make a pedantic point to.

"Ethan, we have a bit of a problem here …".

The reply was typical of the promoter.

"Hang on let me find somewhere less noisy." It did sound like he was at a twenty-first birthday party but actually Ethan was relaxing with his family, including his father, having a lazy Sunday roast at one of their favourite eateries.

A few seconds later the cacophony was no longer to be heard and a sterner voice was emanating out of Stephen's phone, "Right you've got my attention so what exactly is the problem?"

With a gulp of air, as if he was about to dive to the bottom of a swimming pool Stephen began to recount the events of the preceding few hours and just as Ricky had told him earlier.

***

Amanda awoke on Monday morning before her alarm sounded. She hated that but peering at the time on her bedside clock that glowed 05:39 she debated closing her eyes for the remaining six minutes of sleep. Rumpole purred having felt his mistress stir. Amanda located the cat with her left hand and rubbed his fur. Now awake and actually feeling alert for the week ahead Amanda was up, showered, dressed and with a protein shake in her branded smoothie cup she was out the door at a few minutes before 630am. Seconds later her keys jangled at the door as she headed back to her desk to collect her laptop. Rumpole watched her as she strode across the living room with a curious roll of his furry head. He meowed hopeful of a second breakfast, but Amanda turning back towards her door cut off his chances straightaway with a, "No chance my Plumpy Rumpy".

Chambers' ornate entrance had the names of its former Head of Chambers carved into its curved archway together with their dates and Amanda had many times stood and read some of the inscriptions 'Archibald Geraghty Q.C. 1892-1913' 'Benedict

Carruthers 1913-1933' were two of the many names that always resonated with her. The former was instructed to appear before Lord Mersey's hearing into the sinking of the Titanic and the latter was one of the most fervent of advocates of women's suffrage. Amanda would often wonder in awe of what times they must have been in which to practice law. The incumbent Head of Chambers, Rufus Hetherington-Jones, was not so revered by her or indeed anyone for many reasons, but high up on the lengthy list would be that he liked to remind all and sundry that they walked beneath him daily.

Amanda was, as usual, in demand from the minute she arrived. Dave called out to her without even setting eyes on her. It was as if he could distinguish her footsteps from the numerous others on the marble flooring of Chambers' lavish reception. "Miss when you have a moment, I'd like to talk to you about a new instruction."

"One minute Dave please," was Amanda's professional and courteous reply from the extravagant hallway as she rifled through her bursting pigeon-hole. Not that she could have possibly seen Dave's reaction through the walls into the clerk's room, but he had held up a finger and ostentatiously tapped his faux-Breitling watch as if he was counting down the minute. Dave was a very old school barrister's clerk; part of his job was the socialising with the criminal solicitor's firms who instructed his barristers. This meant spending large parts of his working week in various pubs across London and this 'vital' work was only capable of being undertaken by him and him alone. There was no doubt that Dave was the real driving force behind Hartington Chambers rise up the legal directorates and while he never said it out loud he was more than just a little bit peeved in having to walk under Rufus Hetherington-Jones' name every morning, considering he did the square root of fuck all in bringing in the cases.

It was less than a minute, not by much but less than a minute nevertheless, when Amanda glided into the clerks' office. Dave rose to his feet out of respectful habit. The other clerks joined him but the last one to rise was a fresh-faced junior by the name of Jimmy but rather embarrassingly he managed to get the buttons on the cuffs of his Daz white shirt tangled in the cord of his phone so whilst still trying to finish his phone call he was crouched over the table as the trapped wire was not quite long enough to allow him to fully stand unimpeded.

"Did you say you had a new instruction for me Dave?" began Amanda whilst professionally overlooking Jimmy's comedic turn.

"I did Miss, a cheeky little brief for you and it could well be the start of a promising relationship for you and Chambers." This was a typical opening gambit from the senior clerk; it was always the case that could unlock a lot more work. The use of the word brief had no reference to the amount of papers but was an archaic but universally accepted way of referring to the formal paper-based instruction of a barrister.

Amanda was busy but she was astute enough to know that when the senior clerk wanted her to take a case on it was not really a request. However, before Amanda could physically get her hands on the documents the Head of Chambers sauntered in. Jimmy had managed to untangle the phone cord from his shirt and was trying to manipulate the loops back into its former and usual shape. Sensing the need not to be last and to get it entirely right this time Jimmy bolted to his feet with a military-esque ramrod straight back and puffed out chest. No one else moved.

"Thank you, James," replied Rufus, "but there is no need for you to stand in my presence for even though I may well be your superior we are but a family."

Crimson with embarrassment Jimmy sat down with distinctly less panache than when he had jumped up a few seconds earlier. Dave, who had not even acknowledged Rufus' entry inwardly groaned at how the Head of Chambers could be so crassly pompous. Amanda did and said nothing. "So, what do you have here then David?" Dave did not attempt to remind him that his name was actually Dave and of course Jimmy had not even thought to admonish his boss that he was not a James.

"Well Sir I was just saying to Miss Buckingham here," at this point Rufus and Amanda nodded their acknowledgement to each other, "that I have secured a very interesting new instruction and…".

The Head of Chambers intervened with a brutal subtlety that only he possessed. "Let me take a look if you will?" It was spoken as a question but not meant as one.

Dave already knew what was going to happen so did Amanda, and if truth be told the only person who didn't who was in the room, was Jimmy.

Rufus took hold of the bundle of documents and he began to flick through them with the aim of looking studious. After a little more than a cursory scan he declared, "It's an interesting one this one David but the matter may well benefit from a more senior member of Chambers accepting the instruction." Dave, now not having physical control, was facing a losing battle and he knew it. Amanda was only too aware of the office politics and the hierarchical nature of the profession to make the point that in fact the instructing firm, upon recommendation and discussion from Chambers' senior clerk, had sought her to take the case on. She therefore conceded without objection and eloquently delivered the required reply. "Well of course Rufus I am sure that if you have capacity it can only be of benefit to the client for you to accept the instruction."

Dave quickly bowed his head as he could not stop an unprofessional smirk from spreading across his clean-shaven face. Amanda, as with everyone at Chambers, knew full well that Rufus had capacity, there was a private joke amongst some members of Chambers that he actually had infinite capacity.

The Head of Hartington Chambers, enjoying the reverence that he mistakenly took as genuine, began to pour over the more intricate details of the brief and with an occasional guttural groan of assent, in order to audibly display to his subordinates that he was in agreement with the case now before him, he began to walk away, papers in hand. This left Dave and Amanda to lock eyes in knowing acceptance of what had just occurred.

Rufus jutted his head back around the wooden door frame, "David, naturally I'll accept this instruction but we will need to discuss fees," and then with a passing comment that came across as more perfunctory than heartfelt he added directly to Amanda, "Sorry about this but I do think this one is more suited to me …". He cut himself off in order not to finish that sentence. He then stepped fully back into the clerks' room with more discernment than he was ever given credit for. He continued, "I didn't mean a man you know," his words stumbled as he spoke, "Look I didn't mean that this case was better suited to me as a man, I mean a male, a chap you know one of those people ... erm ...".

Amanda, to everyone's relief but none more than Rufus' dived in to bring an end to Rufus' fumbling awkwardness.

"Oh no that didn't cross my mind at all. If you feel that this case needs your expertise, then as the Head of Chambers it is absolutely the right decision to make."

You could see Rufus' anxiety levels drop like a stone as moments before he was fearful that he had stumbled into committing an act of sexual discrimination in the workplace.

"Thank you, Amanda, and well said, it is for the client's best interest that we serve after all."

Amanda nodded her agreement and managed to add in Rufus' favourite but still quite appalling adage, "As you always say it is better to have your hand up than out."

Rufus smiled, almost paternally, towards Amanda as he heard his favourite maxim emanate from one of his colleagues, "Indeed," was his single worded reply and with that he tapped the papers against his left shoulder and headed back to his office.

Amanda was left to share a smirk with Dave who eased the moment of awkwardness with a simple and very Dave like remark, "Next one is yours, Miss. I promise."

"Thank you but there is no need – you keep me busy enough as it is. So, to be honest with my week already looking stacked, racked and jacked it is probably a blessing." Amanda was always capable of saying the right thing at the right time and in the right way, a trait that of course the best advocates had but few at Hartington Chambers genuinely possessed.

"Well you know what we call you?" came back Dave.

"Miss," toyed Amanda. She knew full well that her nickname in Chambers was 'AB', and despite it obviously being her initials, it was Trevor Hamper-Houghton who had let slip that the moniker of 'AB' meant 'Awesome Barrister'.

The other clerks were not quite as appropriate. When they'd been in the pubs of Carey Street and Fleet Street on Friday nights giving barristers nicknames and telling each other how 'AB' really stood for "Awesome Boobs". It was a devasting but true indictment of how sexist the legal world could still be at times.

Dave didn't appreciate the way that other male staff 'rated' the female barristers and he never joined in the terrible macho one-liners that others thought were hysterically amusing; "I'd instruct her" was one of the more common ones along with "I'd give her a two-day trial". He knew what 'AB' really meant but in the societal class divide that existed between barristers and the support staff he did nothing to stop this unacceptable behaviour for as Hartington Chambers' senior clerk he could not afford to exclusively align himself with the barristers to the exclusion of the support staff and vice-versa.

"In any event and despite what you say, the next case is definitely yours, okay?" stated Dave in such a way that Amanda did not want to argue with him. As he spoke Dave turned away not in order to avoid further eye contact with Amanda but the small red indicator lights were dancing all over the telephone switchboard and he, like a moth to a flame was drawn to them. The barrister perceptively took that as her cue to leave the clerks to their job.

Amanda, exhibiting her natural elegance stepped back out of the room in the same breezy affable manner that she had demonstrated a few moments before and although she had clearly just lost out on a new case and a fee there was no petulant reaction or public show of displeasure as a few other members of Chambers would have done.

Dave with a handset in either hand was waving his arms to Jimmy and the other clerks like he was conducting a telephonic orchestra but he watched Amanda leave the room and with a nod of professional respect towards her and ignoring the voices that were hitting his ears like hail drops he said to himself, "She really is an awesome barrister."

Amanda was actually feeling slightly annoyed at what had just taken place. She had missed out on a new instruction because her de facto boss had nothing else to do. There was no point in making a scene though as the longer-term consequences of doing so could far outweigh the benefits of standing her ground. Besides Dave had promised her the next case and he never did that, but still it was most unfair what had just happened and she could not help but wonder if Rufus would have done the same thing if it had been Trevor and not her.

Brushing off her irritation like rain drops on a jacket collar she rationalised that anyway she was far too busy in capacity terms to really take another case on. So despite her justifiable annoyance, by the time she had wound her way around the uneven corridors and low ceilings and down to her office, which was the old pump room in the dank depths of Old Square Lincoln's Inn Fields, she had all but forgotten all about it and her mind was back racing about the tasks that lay ahead of her.

Her roommate Trevor was not at his desk in the far corner of the room, but he was evidently in Chambers somewhere as the smell of cooling coffee was immediately obvious as she pushed the heavy door open. Amanda was pleased not to have to speak to him straightaway as although their lunch on Saturday was very pleasant he was such an awkward character to fully understand and she had no desire to dissect their conversation like football pundits after the final whistle. The simple truth was that Amanda had no desire at all for Trevor.

She spent the next few hours engaged in a series of phone calls and email exchanges in readiness for her trials later that week. When Trevor finally returned to his now stone-cold cortado coffee he was carrying several legally constipated textbooks. His roommate did not hear him enter their shared space and it was only when he dumped those heavy books onto his desk that she looked up.

"Trevor," it was not the warmest of openings, "that looks like a lot of reading."

"Well," was the semi-flirtatious, or at least attempted so reply, "not all of us have your superpowers."

Amanda had no intention of continuing that conversation as the thought of Trevor picturing her as a superhero was not one that she wanted to dwell on.

"Can I get you a coffee? I want to head out for lunch now as I've got a con soon." The conference was really at two in the afternoon and at not quite midday it was a bit early for lunch but Amanda was sensing that Trevor wanted a lengthy and in-depth conversation that she neither had the time nor the inclination for.

"Oh, AB that would be most lovely of you; thank you." Trevor used her nickname but was unaware of the clerks alternative meaning.

He had tried to encourage Chambers to refer to him as "THH" but his suggestion had been completely overlooked, much like his proposal of a spin on a wine and cheese night at Chambers, which he pitched as a wine and chess night. It was not well received and did not go ahead.

In the mistaken belief that fancy types of coffee would make him appear more interesting Trevor asked for a cortado. This was an espresso mixed through with warm milk. He didn't even like them, and in fact his heart raced far too quickly if he drank more than two in a day, but he mistakenly thought it sounded debonair when he ordered it so he'd prefer to do that and let it go cold like the one on his desk.

Without taking the bait at all Amanda slipped on her shoes which she had kicked off a few hours before and rising to her feet she pronounced "Cortado it is". She left their shared office without another word. Seconds later she was back declaring in a light-hearted tone "I can't get you a coffee without any money can I" as she went for her jacket pocket. The style of the coat was called 'boyfriend' which amused Amanda when she bought it a few weeks back. The point was not lost on her either that the nearest Trevor would get to being her boyfriend was the coat sharing the stand in their communal office.

As Amanda was heading out of Chambers under the archway she heard "One second Miss". It was Dave. They skipped down the steps together and Dave jumped straight into what he wanted to say.

"I've just had a call from a guy I know and I'm off

to meet him now about a matter that might well be a great fit for you Miss."

"Which pub is it in Dave?"

Laughing Dave confirmed the meeting was taking place at 'Ye Old White Horse'.

"That's the one near The Old Curiosity Shop."

Dave was impressed with Amanda's knowledge of the capital's public houses, "Indeed Miss … do you fancy a drink then?" It felt the natural thing to say however it was not delivered in a tremendously inviting way, but not because Dave didn't want Amanda to come for a drink with him but simply because he was unsure he should be asking her.

"Thank you, Dave, but no, I've got a con this afternoon." Dave nodded his understanding then Amanda added, "but maybe next time." Dave was slightly taken aback by the last few words but tried to dismiss his surprise with a casual, "for sure, I'll let you know when Miss." With that the two parted and went their separate ways.

Dave went straight through Lincoln's Inn Fields and as he walked down the tarmacked pathways dodging those out for an early lunchtime run his mind began to wander with thoughts about trying to get fit. He slipped into following a female jogger as he strode towards the side exit that led towards his destination and other than ogling the bottom shake as she ran Dave didn't give much more serious contemplation to finding his trainers.

He reached the pub fifteen minutes earlier than was required in order that he could drain at least one full pint before the lunch-time drinking could really start.

Amanda headed to High Holborn for her favourite lunch. There was a little independent sushi bar hidden away on the Lincoln's Inn Fields side of that busy thoroughfare and she loved it. As usual she had her usual.

Amanda forgot Trevor's cortado until she was back inside Chambers, but she went back out to a nearby coffee shop and returned to her office with one and a napkin. He was again absent from their office, so she placed the serviette over the plastic lid and its drinking spout to try and keep the contents hot for as long as possible.

Dave was a pint and three-quarters in when he was joined at the bar by his meeting guest. "Can I get you another one mate?" asked Phil Waring. "Nice one mate, yeah another please." Dave was careful not to say a second one as he didn't like to keep an accurate record of the number of alcoholic drinks he imbibed either.

Phil had known Dave for a very long time and was an integral part of his magical and mystical referral network. Phil Waring was not a lawyer, "God no" he would roar when asked if he was. His job title was 'Senior Case Development Officer' and he worked for an Essex based Criminal Defence Solicitors firm called 'Kelly King'. It was a three-partner firm set up back in the 1970's. The triumvirate was completed by a now deceased old soak of a lawyer by the name of Gerald Keen. The practice dropped his name a few years ago as they were fully aware that the move to abbreviating firms' names down to initials was not going to play well with three Ks.

Phil had been with Kelly King his entire professional life. He started out in the mail room, when businesses needed to have one, and he worked his way up the ranks of the support staff and eventually when

Patrick Kelly, the firm's leader and co-founder, suggested he got a few criminal law qualifications under his belt he did so. As it turned out Kelly's faith was rewarded as Phil blossomed into a first-class case officer and the years in the post room reading what came in and out had taught him more than enough anyway.

Phil was, as ever, dressed in a three piece suit with watch chain and a cufflink shirt and as the two men stood at the long wooden bar taking in hefty gulps of their chosen beers the conversation began with the typical idle chit-chat. Dave was entirely comfortable about this as it meant when the work talk started there'd be plenty of time for at least a couple more pints. They talked about this and that and nothing of any real substance, but Dave made sure that they were both well stocked for drinks as they chatted. The rest of the pub was very quiet as it was only just after midday and most people in that area of London tended not to be 'hitting the booze' that early on a Monday.

When Phil started a fresh topic with "So did you catch the fight on Saturday night?" Dave naturally assumed it was still part of the warmup so casually replied.

"Yeah I did as it goes. It wasn't bad but he was always gonna win."

"Mmm," was the response from Phil.

Dave took that as his cue to say more, "They should have fought years ago but they ducked each other for ages. I mean it was a decent scrap but once it had gone past the opening few rounds it was only ever going one way."

Phil didn't seem that interested in Dave's semi-sloshed untrained critique of a boxing contest that was,

41

in actual fact, a vital one given that the winner was now the mandatory challenger for the World Boxing Association's Heavyweight Title with all the money and fame that went along with such an opportunity. Dave, feeling he needed to get Phil back talking, ended his monologue with, "what do you think then?"

"I didn't know whether you had heard the rumours that was all?" All men and Dave in particular loved a little bit of sporting gossip so draining his pint and forgetting to order another he leant in "Nah, what rumours?"

Dave was expecting to hear some salacious story about drugs or brown envelopes stuffed with cash or ladies of the pole involving one of the fighters from the top of the bill bout last Saturday but what he heard instead made him realise that the work talk had begun and he needed to pay attention and quickly.

Phil went through what he had been told about how Ricky O'Ryan, who was a decent prospect of a boxer who had fought on the undercard of the weekend's boxing show at the O2 Arena and how he had spent the night in the cells at Charing Cross Police Station after a brawl at a pub in Covent Garden. Dave's mind was now racing and when Phil had finished, he led with perhaps the most obvious question, "So how did you hear about this so quickly?"

Phil smirked and commented in a very matter of fact tone that, "occasionally certain information is brought to my attention." Dave laughed so loudly that his guffaw echoed around the practically empty saloon. Sensing that there was no real background noise to mask their conversation Dave leant in and in slightly slurred but hushed tone said, "you mean occasionally certain information is bought by you." Phil appreciated the play on words by Dave and smiling he stood back with his arms out and palms facing the low-level ceiling as if he were saying the words, "What me, I don't know what you could possibly mean."

It was true though as Phil would pay handsomely and always in cash for any leads such as this one and it was a closely guarded secret that everyone knew that a phone call from a desk sergeant to Phil's mobile would result in half an inch of ten pound notes being exchanged. When it was a particularly juicy bit of news or lead, the tenners would morph into twenties. There was a rumour, but it was false, that on a single occasion fifties were the value, but Phil did not do anything to quash such a story for obvious reasons.

Dave just needed to clarify one further thing before the conversation could restart. "Forgive me Phil but who the fuck is Ricky O'Ryan anyway? I've never heard of him; he sounds like he is from one of those god-awful Irish boybands." It was Phil's turn to laugh out loud.

"No no no no, not at all. He was fighting all the way down on the undercard of the show on Saturday night." Dave nodded but as he did so, he furrowed his brow with a question that his brain was forming. "So how did you get to be in the know?"

"Well," and Phil paused as he dramatically drained the last few drops of beer from his pint glass with a loud smack of his lips. This very unsubtle hint was acknowledged by Dave. "Sorry mate my round," and he turned to his left and ordered two fresh beers.

Phil nodded his thanks and now his 'drink meter' had been fed the story could continue. "The firm has known Billy Harris for years. He and Patrick Kelly go way back to all that snooker madness of the mid to late

1980's so when I got the heads up about Ricky I got Patrick to give Billy a call and well … the rest is what it is."

Dave joined the dots as quickly as you'd expect him to but after several pints too many for a Monday lunchtime, he might well have joined the dots, but he couldn't see the final picture. Phil's next question didn't help with his cognitive progression.

"So, what do you think?"

Dave paused in the hope that time would yield the right answer. During that interminable silence, the heavy entrance to the pub opened. It was an 'old-school boozer' so there was a brass door chime that sounded every time the door was used. The bell was the noise that Dave needed to wake him from his slumber and the direct comparison to the subject matter was not lost on him either.

"Ding ding, round one," remarked Dave as he pretended to ring a bell with his right hand. "What you need here then Phil is Counsel to defend this Ricky bloke."

"Well no shit Sherlock," was Phil's immediate reply but he continued with, "So do you have anyone at Hartington?"

Another pause but only for effect this time from Dave, "Yeah of course I do." Given the events of earlier at Chambers there was only one name in the senior clerk's head but given the possibility of media exposure he'd have to be careful that others in Chambers didn't try and push themselves forward for a chance in the spotlight.

Phil finished his pint but this time with a quiet and sated expression. "Another?" enquired Dave, "I'm romeo done," came back the Essex-man's response as he borrowed a line from TV's 'Gavin and Stacey'. Dave was secretly pleased too as he was feeling decidedly wobbly after his liquid lunch and all of a sudden, he didn't fancy another drink.

"Right, I need the bloke's name and I want him fully geared up by the end of the day, I can't let Mr Kelly down as he'll have my guts for garters on this one given that SportsSpace and his mate Billy Harris are involved." Dave chose not to pick up on the innate but entirely misplaced misogynistic assumption that he would only recommend a male barrister and so he simply responded with; "Understood and leave this with me. I'm back to my desk now so don't worry." Phil smiled back at his friend, "I'm not worried. I'm not the one that spent the night in the nick!" Dave laughed but this time less exuberantly.

Having settled the bar tab with petty cash from the Chambers' office account Dave led Phil out of the pub and as the doorbell was still chiming behind them, he asked, "So did he do it?" It was the question that no lawyer ever dared to ask for the answer could mean a potential accusation of perjury if the accused declares one thing in private and then another whilst in the dock.

With a shrug of his shoulders Phil coldly replied, "I dunno …," and then having reflected he continued, "but a professional boxer involved in a pub fight doesn't sound good does it?"

Dave grunted his assent but before he could verbally react Phil ended their conversation, "but that's why I called you to sort it out."

"No pressure then," joked Dave.

The two men said their goodbyes and Dave headed straight to the nearest newsagent for a can of full fat

Coca-Cola and a packet of Walkers salt and vinegar crisps. Standing under the shop's awning he expertly gulped down the fizzy pop in one hit and let out a rasping belch that caused at least four passers-by to look at him with disdainful revulsion. Dave then went next door to a typical London street café that sold everything from a full English breakfast to mozzarella stuffed gnocchi. After a burger and chips and a large cappuccino Dave headed back to Chambers with one hand stuffed into his packet of crisps. His earlier vague thought of getting fitter had not gone well.

***

Stephen's phone had not rung for hours. Connor and Michael had long since departed for the airport and the homeward flight back to Belfast. Ricky had messaged his Mum to let her know that he was staying in London a little longer, but he omitted the reason why. 'Okay my Star Man xx' was the last message on his phone.

Sat in their hotel room Ricky was full of questions but Stephen was bereft of answers. The call with Ethan Harris on the Sunday had ended with, "Stay put and I'll get someone to call you tomorrow."

The phone call had come part way through Monday morning. Sat together on the edge of a bed the two men listened to a conversation involving them with a 'Phil Waring'. It was not really a conversation in that no real words were exchanged Phil just rattled out commands such as, "Say nothing," "Do nothing," "Go nowhere," and when Stephen tried to say something he was cut off with a brutal, "we can talk about that when we meet later today." With no consultation whatsoever Mr Waring confirmed that this meeting was going to take place at two-thirty.

Phil, having left Dave outside the pub was immediately on the phone to his boss Patrick Kelly. "Yes, Paddy we'll get a barrister in an hour or so and I am now off to talk to the clients." Patrick's reply was so direct and matter of fact that all Phil could respond with was, "Understood."

There was nothing for Stephen and Ricky to do other than sit and wait. Neither of these two men were overly blessed with patience and the wall-mounted television offered little to distract them as the clock slowly ticked around towards two-thirty. Stephen had earlier manged to extend their accommodation by a night although he had winced with excruciating pain as the unjustifiably excessive charge was added to his sizeable credit card balance.

***

Amanda's phone rang. She was alone, again, in her room but she had not really taken much notice of that fact. Looking up towards Trevor's desk she noticed that the napkin was still gently in place over the coffee cup. As she was on her own, she answered the call by pressing speakerphone. "Miss," came the male voice. "Hey Dave," was her cheerful reply.

"Take me off speaker please Miss." That was a most unlike Dave comment but dutifully she obliged. "Everything alright Dave?" began Amanda with slightly more hesitancy in her voice than normal.

"Of course, Miss but I just need to be sure that this conversation is not accidentally overheard." He paused briefly. "So, you know how I promised you the next case, well I've got it already."

"That's incredibly professional of you of Dave." Amanda's reply made Dave lose his focus slightly; was she being chatty or flirty? Dave shook off this thought with annoyance and carried on. "Thank you, Miss., It's an interesting one but definitely one that is a great fit for you but I need to move quickly and quietly with it as it might be the sort of case that would get others interested." Amanda knew exactly what Dave meant by this. There was only one type of instruction that the clerks ever referred to as 'getting others interested' and that was one with a chance of media attention and a potential slot in front of the news cameras.

Her open response was a leading question, a typical device used by barristers to get more from the answer than a simple yes or no. "I understand Dave." Amanda picked up the phone and the speaker was immediately disconnected. "Tell me all about it."

Amanda, as she always did, grabbed a fresh Counsel notepad from a stack to her left. As she bent down her lucky charm, an ankle bracelet, caught her eye and it gave her an immediate sense that her notes on this case were going to be important. How important of course she didn't know at the time.

Handset cradled between her right ear and shoulder as she swept a free bit of space for her notepad, she seized the nearest pen and began to scribble down some of the information Dave was hurtling in her direction.

Amanda had, as ever, more questions than Dave could answer but he reassured her that those instructing her would be providing a full and detailed brief later. Amanda trusted Dave, there was no reason not to and when it came to fees Dave stated that it would be her usual rate. "Okay and thank you," was all that could be said to that.

Before the private conversation came to its natural conclusion the door to the room burst open and in strode a euphoric Trevor Hamper-Houghton. He stomped into the centre of the room – the self-described 'no persons land' between the occupants' respective desks. Amanda had no issue with it being dubbed 'no man's land' as that was always what such spaces were called but Trevor, ever the champion of pointless causes insisted. Trevor's arms were outstretched, and he had that self-congratulatory look across his clean shaven but blotchy face that resembled the cat that had got the cream. Amanda smiled at him indifferently and gave him the universally accepted single index finger raise whilst holding the receiver to indicate that she'd be done in a matter of seconds. Trevor pirouetted in a far too competent way as he span away from her to face his all but empty desk.

"Thanks so let's catch up when you know more," declared Amanda. Dave ended their call with a, "Thank you Miss."

Even before the line had been disconnected inside their shared office Trevor was heaping praise upon himself. "Amanda let me tell you about some cracking news." There was no pause as he bolted on, "So there I was telling Rufus my thoughts on another evening shindig for Chambers when I got the tap!"

Amanda had not really been paying much attention but hearing the words 'got the tap' made her shoot back in her seat as if a seatbelt had yanked her back at the moment of impact. She stared intently into his eyes. Her immediate reaction was 'surely not, god no, please no… there is no way he of all people has had 'the tap' to indicate that his application to take silk and join the luminary ranks of Queen's Counsel would be favourably received.

Trevor saw the mix of astonishment and terror in Amanda's reaction and he waded straight in, "Oh no AB I didn't mean that tap I meant that a really juicy brief had just been earmarked for me!"

Amanda's sheer relief was palpable but as ever she effortlessly recovered her poise and said to Trevor, "Well done you, that is fantastic news." She really meant it too as despite his professional limitations as a barrister and his bumbling awkwardness as a man he deserved his share of good fortune.

Amanda, even with Rufus Hetherington-Jones all but poaching cases and all that this meant for her, would never be envious of others and their successes, after all as her Uncle would often tell her 'good things happen to good people'. She had adapted that slightly to 'good cases happen to good barristers' and of course she had just had her little slice of good news with her call from Dave so there was no need to 'rain on Trevor's parade' and it was so nice to see him so enthused.

Trevor was shuffling his feet from side-to-side and bobbing his head up and down and left to right and Amanda thought for a moment that he was dancing at a silent disco. Then in front of her, as if performing a routine, he clenched his hands to make two fists and he started throwing air punches. He was shadow boxing of all things realised Amanda and what a strange thing to be doing, she mused.

The alarm on her mobile broke the charade before her and she grabbed it with relief and noted that the time had come for her conference. Amanda hastily departed, bundles and computer in hand leaving

Trevor to exclusively continue enjoying his elative moment. As the door closed, he slumped back against his desk completely out of breath and red faced and gasping heavily for air. He could not fathom how anyone could last that level of activity for twelve rounds of three minutes.

After a very successful conference with instructing solicitors regarding a complicated case relating to allegations of cyber-crime and crypto currency exchanges Amanda returned to her room and was blissfully greeted with the emptiness of the space. After an hour or so churning through the electronic mountains of emails she called it a day and headed home for a well-earned hot bath and early night.

**

Stephen was sat, mouth agog as Phil Waring espoused a whole host of commands. Halfway through this monologue it occurred to Stephen that the way Phil was directing what needed to be done and also what should not be done he'd actually make an excellent cornerman. Ricky sat motionless throughout in a cheap egg-shaped plastic chair in the corner of the hotel lobby. It was not really a corner of the lobby, as there was little more than just a few feet of spare space between the entrance and the reception counter but nevertheless Phil had commandeered three of these seats; although as he quipped spikes would have been more comfortable. He had made a little triumvirate up against two flanks of the interior hotel walls. He had then dragged a side table of leaflets and flyers of London attractions from its usual place between a dying pot plant and an almost empty fire extinguisher and placed that between the runway from door to welcome desk in order to block off as much interruption or prying ears as possible.

Phil's last touch was to place himself facing into the room and therefore Stephen and Ricky were looking at the badly whitewashed walls which possessed no eyes nor ears but just a few more than a handful of potted imperfections where the paint had not been distributed evenly.

As Phil was explaining the complexities of what had occurred and why immediate and ideally 'hush hush' action was needed his mobile phone began to vibrate. He shifted to his left and thrust his signet ring bejewelled hand into his right trouser pocket and eventually after one or two mighty jerks his iPhone plus finally squeezed itself from its fabric hollow. "Sorry chaps this is the barrister's clerk I was telling you about", he stated. He was not looking for any permission to be granted it was a statement of fact that he was going to answer the call but submissively both Ricky and Stephen nodded their acceptance.

"Talk to me Dave," Phil barked into the phone.

On the other end of the line Dave played along as he knew that Phil liked to be in charge when he could, and this was one of those times. "Simple Phil – Amanda Buckingham is the one and she is already primed and ready."

"I don't care if she is greased up and waiting for basting Dave I specifically asked for a fucking bloke." Dave cut him off before Phil could utter any further outlandish proclamations, "She is the best and to be honest you are a mug if you don't get her on your team. She's never lost and has no intention of doing so."

After a glance at the screen to tell him that normal

office hours were dwindling away for that Monday and the prospects of having to go back to his boss at Kelly King and say that there was no barrister retained on the grounds of his pathetic sexual bias meant that Phil, and to re-establish his assumed dominance, went back with, "It's your call and your neck on the line."

"No doubts at this end," stated Dave with full confidence. He meant it as well and the pitch and tone of those five words resonated in Phil's ear, "Fair enough she gets a chance." At the other end of the line Dave rolled his eyes.

Phil then coldly but boldly affirmed, "we will talk fees later," and he didn't even wait for a reply as he terminated the call. Dave with a snort of disbelief hung up the receiver and went on with the rest of his hectic afternoon.

Phil went back to the two statues sat before him. "Right we have a barrister – she is the dogs bollocks apparently, so next stage is dealing with the interview at the cop shop."

Ricky found his voice, "What's going to happen?" his Northern Irish accent masked the worry in his words.

Phil shuffled a few inches closer and hunching forward as he crouched, his head naturally lowered towards his knees. He went searching for Ricky's emerald eyes and when he found them, he smiled and reassuringly spoke with a much lighter air, "So Ricky first thing is volunteering yourself back to the station for a formal interview. After that it really should get tossed out but who knows what the Crown Prosecution Service will do but do not worry, SportsSpace and this Amanda barrister bird will be with you all the way."

"So will I," Stephen declared as robustly as he could.

Ricky let out a sigh that seemed to be all the breath he had in his body.

"So, what's this going to cost?" asked Stephen. With that Ricky shot a glance to his right. It hadn't even occurred to him what this might end up costing him. As quickly as he looked at Stephen his gaze returned to Phil.

"Nothing," came the reply. This time it was Stephen who let out an audible deep sigh of relief. "You are part of the SportsSpace family," continued Phil, "and I've spoken to both Billy and Ethan over the last few hours and our costs and those of the barrister are picked up by them." He paused for effect, "unless of course you've gone totally Tonto on us then you're out and on your own." It didn't really matter that it was not Phil who had conversed with the Harriss, but it certainly made him sound as if he was sitting at the top table. The reality was Phil would probably be serving it rather than sitting at it but felt good to claim he was on first name terms with the bosses at SportsSpace.

"Everything we've said to you and Ethan is 100% bang on," announced Stephen with newfound confidence now that he knew his overweight credit card was not going to get another physical examination.

Ricky nodded but Phil was unsure, so he pressed "Everything okay Ricky?"

"Yeah of course totally. I mean not that everything is okay obviously but for sure 100% bang on," was the slightly reticent response. Phil said nothing but there was something in how Ricky spoke that made him faintly curious.

Phil moved on explaining that he was going to arrange a voluntary appearance at Charing Cross Police Station the next morning. Stephen interjected almost before he had heard those words, "Hang on a mo… you mentioned that earlier but what the hell does that mean?"

Phil had never ever in all of his years at Kelly King experienced any client who was not worried about going to a police station. It was a completely natural reaction to what most people would consider to be an alien environment but to Phil it was his second home. He knew every trick and trade craft there was and therefore was able to speak with utter confidence, "Right that's the first decent question you've asked." Stephen and Ricky performed a synchronised shuffle in readiness for what they heard next.

"Voluntary attendance means you are not being arrested and you are just helping the police with their enquiries and investigation. You are free to leave at any time, but it is about tackling the issue head on. After all, the aim of the game is to get this thing dropped asap and get you back home."

"Yeah," came the mutual response. Ricky added "spot on that."

Phil continued, "So I'll see you tomorrow first thing and I'll have the team together."

"What do I say?" asked Ricky

"As little as possible," came the immediate retort from Phil. "Leave that to me and the barrister."

Phil's confidence, which was bordering on arrogance, was infectious and most reassuring for both Ricky and Stephen. As the three men talked through a few possible scenarios they all began to feel more and more confident about their plans for the next day.

When their conversation came to a close, they exchanged handshakes and a few small pleasantries. Phil then declared that he wanted to update the rest of the team and his final words to Ricky were delivered in a matter of fact way that despite being obvious landed with a similar weight to the punch that had knocked out Kris 'The Sleep Maker' Baker. "Get a decent night sleep as it's a big day tomorrow." With that Phil left the hotel and didn't look back as he was straight onto his phone whilst trying to hail a black cab to get him back to Liverpool Street Station.

There was nothing left for Ricky and Stephen to do but to return to the sanctuary of their hotel room and await the morning. Ricky didn't sleep well in part due to the horrendous snoring from his roommate but also because his mind could not settle for the fear of the unknown that was awaiting him.

Phil's first conversation after leaving the hotel was to Dave informing him, although it was a command not a request, that Amanda was needed tomorrow morning for an early conference. Even before Dave could check availability Phil had moved on to his next call as he updated Patrick Kelly. Phil had hoped that he would then be asked to update Ethan and Billy Harris at SportsSpace personally, but his boss told him that he'd do that. Phil was slightly grumpy about that as he was rather hopeful of the chance to speak to those two VIPs of the sporting world.

***

Amanda was at home when the call came in from Dave. She was working, as always, by reviewing her notes from that afternoon's conference but as ever she answered the phone to Chambers' senior clerk. "Miss sorry to disturb, but you are needed for a conference with instructing solicitors on that new case tomorrow morning." Amanda opened her online diary and noted that she had booked Rumpole in to have his claws clipped at the vets at 0900. "No worries Dave. I'm good for that." Dave, as with all clerks, had access to the shared diary folders of the barristers at Hartington Chambers so he was already aware that there was no court or meeting commitments but he needed to check that Amanda was content to re-schedule her trip to the vets.

It was notable straight away to Dave that this conversation lacked the usual repartee so, sensing that there was nothing else that needed to be said, he ended the conversation with, "I will email the details and timings later."

Amanda had been looking forward to taking Rumpole to the vets. Getting a cat's claws clipped was something that she was perfectly capable of doing herself with a pair of nail clippers and some heavyweight cat treats as bribery. The reality was though that she liked the look of the vet. Ben was the sort of man that would attract a lot of attention in a bar, at the gym or even standing on the platform waiting for a train. The fact that he cared for animals and dressed like a doctor made him all but irresistible to every woman that he came into contact with. Every woman with perhaps the odd exception. Amanda was that exception and she found that to be really quite odd. He liked her of that she was certain. Ben had been fantastic after Rumpole had a little health scare recently and they'd even gone out to the theatre shortly after the cat had got the all clear but as with so much in her personal life there were a lot of promising beginnings but, to date, no happy ever afters. Amanda really wanted to fall for him but there was something missing, she could not work out what that was but hopefully the more time spent with him would dissipate her nagging reservation. Annoyingly though she was going to have to reschedule seeing him tomorrow and of course getting Rumpole's claws trimmed.

Hunting for her mobile phone was a game that Amanda played a lot and she was patting down papers, opening folders, and checking pockets once more. Frustrated she gave up her search and walked to a side table and the landline telephone. Other than her Aunt and Uncle who called every Wednesday at eight in the evening no one else used it and Amanda was not even sure why she still had it but the slick salesman from Sky explained that it was linked to the broadband package, so the cordless telephone and stand remained but it might as well have been decorative for the amount of use it got. Amanda dialled her mobile number into the handset and waited hoping that the receiving device was not turned to silent. Ring ring … Ring ring. Then she heard the all too common 'opening' ring tone from an iPhone. It was the tune that almost everyone else seemed to use so that inevitably when it began there was a race of those in earshot to establish if it was their phone that was ringing or not. Amanda followed the sound towards her cream three-piece sofa. Rumpole was sprawled as he often was on the centre cushion but stretched just enough so he was touching the other two. He was proudly telling anyone who came within sitting distance that this was his territory.

Amanda carefully checked under all of the ludicrous

amount of scatter cushions at each end of the sofa. Rumple didn't move an inch. She then pushed the flat of her hand down each edge to find nothing but a hair clip and a Lindt chocolate wrapper. This time Rumpole overextended his position to try and remind his mistress that he was in charge but moving as he did Amanda saw the edge of her phone. That fat cat had snuggled up to it because it was like a little hot water bottle. "Oh Rumpy you are such a silly little cat," teased Amanda. "You've had me looking all over for my phone and all this time you were giving it a cuddle!" Rumpole gave up his personal heater with little fuss as it was replaced with a generous amount of tummy-rubs.

The screen on her phone indicated seven new emails, two messages and one other notification about a software update and a missed call. The missed call was from an 0207 number, but no name had been stored against it. No wonder no one ever uses the landline thought Amanda when she herself didn't even have it stored as one of her contacts.

The emails were all work related. Not a single spam or advertising one which, given the amount of online retail therapy Amanda engaged in was a surprise. One of those seven emails was from Dave confirming the details for tomorrow's meeting. She would read and reply to that shortly. The two messages were both from her Aunt and both exactly the same *We have tickets for the Opera on Wednesday so we will call this Thursday at 8pm. Lots of love. AE. Xx*

No worries. Have a wonderful time at the Opera. Looking forward to catching up Thursday xx was the simple but effective reply sent.

The other message was from the contact she had

saved as 'Ben the Vet'. That in itself was indicative of how Amanda really felt about him despite his handsome appearance – it was a professional relationship. She opened the message, "Looking forward to seeing you and Rumpole tomorrow. B."

Amanda was slightly saddened that she now had to message him to cancel the appointment and she was inwardly pleased that she was disappointed. Maybe there was hope after all. A few drafts later she settled on sending 'Sadly no can do as I've got an important meeting. I will re-book soon'. The first version didn't have the word important in it but Amanda felt that she needed to add it in so Ben didn't think she was re-scheduling for something that wasn't and also it had "I promise" after "soon" but having ruminated for way too long over those two words she took them out. She also sent a much more detailed and formal email to the automated booking system at the veterinary practice.

***

The following morning came to Amanda much like every other. Her routine and that of Rumpole's had been established early on and pretty much religiously adhered to from then. There was nothing particularly different about this one but as Amanda was watching her Nespresso Aeroccino froth and fizz up her milk she could not help sensing a niggling misgiving that her world may well be turned upside down and back to front.

She was early for her pre-arranged meeting with Phil Waring of Kelly King Solicitors. Dave as directed in his email of last night had booked one of the smaller conference rooms at Hartington Chambers. It was a little early for most barristers to be in their rooms or milling around the lobby in the hope that someone would overhear, and perhaps more importantly believe, how busy they were or how well their practice was going.

Amanda had met many Phil's before. She knew the type from the moment he had sat down and adjusted his pocket watch silver chain-link. Phil starting off by telling her what to do and how to think and why she should listen to him. Her tactic with such people, and they always tended to be men, was to just let them talk themselves quiet as her time would come soon enough.

Eventually, having repeated himself at least twice on every point or recommendation or directive he had uttered, Phil became, as Amanda knew he would, exasperated and speechless. All that he had left was "I hope you say more when you are in Court."

Amanda smiled at him. Not a pleasant 'nice to see you' beam or even a suggestive 'yes you may come and talk to me' grin but a 'shut up it's my turn now' smile.

"Thank you, Phil," it was brutal as the way she said it left no doubt that she didn't mean it. "I've heard what you think and how you want to move forward but having heard what you've said, speaking to Dave and carefully considering the matter I would suggest that we do not attend the police station, a noble plan but at this stage not a prudent one."

Amanda then set out six reasons, all more salient than the one that went before on why having Ricky O'Ryan voluntarily submitting to a police interview 'at this immediate stage', those four words were stressed heavily as she spoke, was not a sensible course of action.

Phil tried to argue his way through the first two. He

struggled. The next three he was not sure he really understood enough to debate them and the final one, which was conceivably the easiest to rebuff, he simply failed to address the simplicity of it as it ran through his brain.

Number six was coldly delivered by Amanda with the curt clipped tone that landed with the force of any boxer's best punch. "Without knowing what the CPS intend to do there is an inherent risk to Mr O'Ryan in appearing voluntarily." She followed up this sage guidance with further rock-solid advice "I would actually consider that the next course of action is to establish where the mindset of the CPS is, for if they are looking at proceeding then the likelihood of the Police detaining him goes up."

"Okay," thought Phil "she's smart," and Dave was right, and he also considered that "having a woman defend a boxer might well gain some sympathy down the line."

He replied to all of Amanda's six points with a highly unsuccessful attempt at being blasé "If you think that's the way to play it for now then so be it." Inwardly Phil was impressed but externally he desperately tried to portray that he was still in charge. Amanda allowed Phil to believe his fallacy; after all they both knew who was now in charge.

"So, what's next?" spluttered Phil. He tried to sound commanding but the more he tried the less effect he actually had.

"A meeting with Ricky." It was more of a decree than a suggestion, but she was acutely aware that Phil liked the notion of making the final call. "I would recommend with your consent of course," she spoke softly but full of confidence as if she were a snake charmer playing a swaying tune to make the serpent dance.

"I think," Phil paused as if he was deliberating hard "a meeting now is probably the most reasoned strategy." He looked directly at Amanda who nodded her assent.

Phil reached for his phone that he had placed screen down on the conference table.

Amanda collected up her notes and heard one side of the ensuing conversation as brief as it was. "Stephen, me and the barrister are heading over to you. See you in twenty." With that the red button of termination was thumbed and Phil rose from his seat and headed for the door and even before Amanda had the chance to finish packing her Oxblood natural leather Mulberry shoulder bag he was away down the corridor.

There was no need to rush after him as Phil had turned the wrong way. So, Amanda neatly rearranged the chairs as the door closed. Scanning the room to make sure it was more than presentable for its next occupant she grasped the brass door handle and pulling it towards her she was greeted with the sight of Phil pounding the thick grey carpet back to whence he had just come.

Professionally but with a hint of satisfaction Amanda ushered Phil to his left with a "This way is quicker." Phil said nothing and as they left Chambers and walked the short distance to their destination, the two people exchanged nothing more than the barest of civilities.

***

Back in his office Trevor Hamper-Houghton was energetically pressing letters on his keyboard and staring at the screen for the results of his internet searches. He stumbled over a website that had the records of professional boxers. He located the search function and typed in 'Ricky O'Ryan'. The results that Trevor read looked impressive as there were six green blocks against his name to indicate six wins and therefore a perfect record. Ricky's date of birth and hometown were also provided along with his opponents. The barrister noted the date of his last bout being the Saturday just gone and the location as the O2 Arena, London. Trevor withdrew his head from the computer screen as he was there that night, but he didn't recall anyone by the name of O'Ryan fighting Baker. After a few more tortuously inaccurate searches he came across the fight schedule and he located 'Ricky O'Ryan -v- Kris Baker' but with a time of TBA and given that it was the second fight on a lengthy undercard Trevor now realised why he had not seen the contest as he wasn't there that early.

Reaching for the telephone he punched in the internal code for the clerk's room. He waited and he lost count of the rings he heard until eventually Jimmy answered.

"Who is this?" was his rather uninspiring opening.

"Jimmy," came the reply.

"Ah James," led in Trevor "can you dial me into Lorna Williams at the CPS."

There was no "please."

"Yes of course Sir."

Trevor disengaged that conversation by taking the handset away from his right ear as his left hand idly flicked the nails that only a few days before had been expertly manicured at a salon in Sloane Square. It occurred to him as he sat there looking at Ricky O'Ryan's boxing record and how easy it was to access it, as to whether he could develop a similar website for barristers. He decided to add this to his memory bank and to raise it the next time he was in conversation with Rufus.

His earpiece resonated with the sound of a connection to an outside line and less than two rings later Trevor heard the unmistakable Welsh accent of Lorna Williams.

She began with "THH," and Trevor swelled with pride that his earlier efforts at promoting his initials as a nickname were working. He had pressed Lorna in their previous call, when she asked how he preferred to be addressed, to use 'THH'; Lorna was expecting perhaps 'Mr Hamper-Houghton' or Trevor but she was happy to play along.

"I just want to follow up on our call," began Trevor "Uh huh," was all he got in reply. Undeterred he bounded onwards "I am so pleased that you were directed to instruct me in relation to this matter." That was a bit of stretch thought Lorna as she had been directed to Hartington Chambers by her boss and when asking for available barristers the reply from a clerk, whose name she didn't recollect, and apparently the involvement of its Head, Rufus Hetherington-Jones, who of course she knew by reputation was that Mr Trevor Hamper-Houghton had availability. It was not necessarily the most auspicious of recommendations that a barrister had capacity at such short notice.

Lorna continued to listen to Trevor's monologue of how he was preparing to advise the CPS on an ongoing basis but she was not entirely enamoured by his repetitive references to 'establishing a relationship that can lead to further instructions'.

Sensing that he was doing all of the talking Trevor opted for a brief recap "So as it currently stands the position the CPS are intending, at this stage, to move forward with a prosecution against Mr Ricky O'Ryan and having had the opportunity to carefully consider our discussion earlier it may be that a charge of GBH with intent is how you wish to proceed?" There was not enough inflection in Trevor's tone to denote that he had asked a question but as he stopped speaking there was enough of a pause for Lorna to realise that she was required to reply.

"Thank you ... er ... THH ...," She stumbled slightly to correctly use his initials. "As is often the case with these types of matters we liaise with the Police and the officers involved to correctly identify that we have enough grounds to proceed and it would appear having read the file that we are looking to move against Mr O'Ryan and with you as prosecuting counsel we would hope to achieve an expedited trial and a conviction at that level."

Grievous Bodily Harm with intent to cause GBH was at the more severe end of the Offences Against the Person Act of 1861 and carries with it a maximum sentence of life imprisonment as it is the intent to commit grievous bodily harm that elevates such a charge from the slightly less serious charge of GBH which has a maximum penalty of five years.

The two debated the facts a little more and agreed that it would be interesting to see if O'Ryan volunteered himself to submit to a formal interview with the Police as Lorna thought would happen, as then a charge could be presented and a listing could occur at the Magistrates Court. Trevor commented that "That would of course depend on whether he has representation or not and of course whom that might be."

There was no way he could have known that the barrister he was referring to was actually his roommate.

***

Amanda and Phil met Stephen and Ricky not in the lobby this time but in the hotel room. It's two occupants had done their best to tidy up and make the beds but they were not chambermaids nor had either of them served in the military so their efforts would not have met with praise from either a hotel manager or a drill sergeant.

"I am sorry that we have to meet here but it is the best place to have a private conversation with all of us," was Phil's opener.

Amanda was entirely unsure why there was a need for such a 'cloak and dagger' approach. The only viable reason, to her acute mind at least, was that it was better to adopt a cautious attitude from the get-go as even if Ricky O'Ryan was not a 'box-office name' his promoters certainly were.

"Am I going for this interview thing then?" enquired Ricky with more than a little trepidation in his voice.

"I am glad you brought that up," waded in Phil. "Counsel and I," he thumbed an acknowledgment to Amanda who had set up a temporary work station on the corner of the ledge sized desk in the room. "chatted this through earlier and actually before we do anything, we need to understand a little more about which way the police are going to go with it." Before he could explain what, he meant Ricky, now visibly worried, couldn't hold back in interrupting "Hang on, what does 'which way the police are going to go' actually mean?"

Phil shuffled his backside on the corner of the bed and in doing so he only ruffled up the sheets which had not been fully tucked under the mattress.

This type of situation was where Amanda showed how competent and capable, she was. "If I may?" she said gently but with real authority. All eyes turned to her and she caught a glimpse of relief in Phil's.

"As Phil rightly alluded to, we need to ensure that what we do next as a team is the best for Ricky." She smiled at Ricky – not a feigned smile for a social media selfie but a warm confidence inspiring one. Ricky nodded back for her to continue. Stephen was listening attentively and showed no signs of wanting to say anything and Phil was trying to look eager but his mouth was tightly shut and he was not giving the impression he had any intention of opening it anytime soon.

"So perhaps at this stage and until we know whether the Police and the CPS are going to move forward or not it might well be more prudent to carefully consider a range of options."

"CPS?" asked Stephen

"Sorry yes Stephen, the CPS stands for Crown Prosecution Service which is the organisation that proceeds with criminal cases in the UK. It is made up of fourteen regional offices and Westminster is where we are." No one said anything. Amanda, sensing that there was not a great deal of interest in her detailed description of the CPS, concluded with "The CPS is an independent body, independent of the police, and so it decides, albeit in consultation, whether to bring a case to Court or not."

A pause followed and still no-one, not even Phil, made any effort to comment.

"So if we can establish what the CPS' objectives are then we, as a team," Amanda made a square with her index fingers as she spoke to encapsulate all four of them "can decide whether or not we need to attend the police station voluntarily or under caution."

"Phil, can you find out who is leading up the matter at the CPS and whether they've retained Counsel as that'll be the best guide as to their plans moving forward?"

"What can I do?" asked Ricky.

Amanda turned slightly to face him and smiling again she spoke clearly and firmly "You need to tell me everything that happened on Saturday night."

Nodding his agreement Ricky coughed to clear his throat in readiness to tell the events for one more time.

"I've heard it all before so I am going to step out to make some calls to see what I can find out," declared Phil as he made the few steps to the door. "Thanks Phil," said Amanda but he didn't hear her or if he did, he didn't acknowledge it as his phone was already pressed to his ear as the door closed behind him.

Amanda waited for a brief moment before directing her attention to both Stephen and Ricky "Okay so what I'd like from you is the full details of everything. I know you've already gone though it at least once with Phil but I need to hear everything from your point of view in order that I can give you the best help and advice I can". She then added in a more deliberate tone something that she wouldn't normally say "and this includes anything that you might have forgotten or overlooked to mention to Phil."

Ricky and Stephen exchanged puzzled looks and Stephen spoke first "Amanda we have nothing to hide and we've told Phil everything."

"Everything," he added once more. Amanda nodded her understanding and repeated that single word but this time she looked directly at Ricky "Everything." Ricky moved his head up and down but only slightly and it seemed, to Amanda's trained intuition, that this duo may well have differing interpretations of the word 'everything'.

Ricky was carefully remembering the events of last Saturday and at times Amanda had to politely ask Stephen not to interject as she was concerned that Stephen was trying too hard to coach him. Given though that he was Ricky's trainer and manager it was perhaps an obvious thing to offer and Amanda clearly identified that the relationship between these two men was more akin to father and son than just trainer and fighter.

***

Back in Chambers Trevor was content with how the call had gone earlier with Lorna and the CPS. The only negative, as he saw it, was that she ended their conversation with a "Thanks Trev lets catch up tomorrow."

His email account was boxed full of unread emails from various travel sites, wine merchants and department stores. Interspersed amongst this catalogue of spam was the occasional work one, the last being from Lorna. Last was the correct description but it was the only work email in his inbox that day so first and last would have been a more accurate definition.

The electronic message started well as it was addressed to THH. The rest of the email was cursorily scanned by its recipient as it reconfirmed his instruction and it again set out the expectations of the CPS. Trevor had no real concerns given that the assailant had been seen drinking heavily and was identified by the victim as the person who threw the punch and, most importantly for the prosecution's case, he was also a professional boxer. There didn't seem much to argue about and surely whoever was advising the O'Ryan chap just needed to take it on the chin and move on. The unintended boxing pun made him chuckle out loud with laughter. Looking up from his screen he had hoped to share his joke with Amanda, but she was not at her desk.

***

Amanda was in fact still frantically scribbling into her light blue Counsel's note pad. She had given up on the desk as it was barely wide enough to balance her pen let alone write on so she was using her right thigh and right hand to steady the page as her left scrawled down as much of the information as she could as it was tumbling out of the mouths of Ricky and Stephen. It was as if a dam had burst and as fast as Amanda could transcribe, she was no secretary with short hand skills, but she didn't want them to stop opening up to her for she feared as soon as Phil came back from his calls they'd stop talking as quickly as if someone had switched off a light.

Sure enough when Phil drummed the side of his right fist against her door four or five times the echoes in the room made everyone jump and the two men became noticeably more on edge. After Amanda had jumped to her feet and opened the door Ricky and Stephen became as withdrawn and uncommunicative as two boys caught with their fingers in the cookie jar.

Phil didn't read the room at all. It was not his skill set. Into Amanda's head leapt a Churchillian quote that seemed to sum up Phil perfectly "The only bull I know who carries his own china shop around with him." She couldn't remember who Churchill said it about, but she'd ask her Uncle on Thursday during their rearranged weekly chat as he'd know for sure. It was such a perfect depiction of Phil as he stood huffing and puffing in the cramped hotel room that was barely built big enough for two let alone four.

Two of the three men looked sullen but the third was ostensibly desperate to speak. Amanda realised that with the bullish Phil in the room there was little more she was going to gain from Ricky and Stephen so asked "How have you got on?" but it came out a little more curtly than she'd have preferred.

Phil shot an irritated look Amanda's way and for a moment he thought about calling her on what he took to be her unnecessary tone but then he quickly rationalised that it might be one of those times where 'the reds were at home' and he had no time for that bullshit. So other than letting her know he'd picked up on her tone by giving her a shitty look he burst into forceful dialogue.

"Right then there's good and bad news." Normally when people say that phrase or a derivation of it the speaker then asks for which one the listener would like first but that did not happen as Phil bounded on "Good news is that its Lorna Williams at the CPS on this one, she is pretty decent and I can work with her. I also spoke to someone 'in the know'," he didn't expand on that and frankly Amanda was relieved he hadn't "and apparently the police have got a witness statement from the bloke that got punched but I don't know what's in it and also there is some grainy CCTV footage." Thankfully he got to the good news as Ricky was beginning to sweat more than he had done in the boxing ring last Saturday night "so their case against Ricky is 'not all that strong' from an evidential point of view."

Phil took a giant gulp of stale hotel room air that actually made him cough and splutter. He had the manners to get a hand to his mouth just in time and in doing so he did not see Ricky and Stephen exchange worrying looks as if they were saying "If that is the good news then what the fuck is the bad stuff!"

After clearing his throat Phil pressed on "So the bad news is that my 'contact' says that they've instructed counsel, but he didn't know who it was." When he said contact, he raised and closed his index and middle finger on both hands to perform the universally recognised quotation symbols. Amanda was unsure why he did that as it made no sense whatsoever and Phil was not to know that the inaccurate use of air quotes was literally one of the things that infuriated her the most. Although to Amanda's credit, and having already ruffled his feathers with her tone, she let this one go. It still annoyed her though.

"So, what does the bad news actually mean then as speaking for Ricky and me we are more than a little confused?" said Stephen.

Phil had decided he'd spoken enough, and he had disengaged from the room and was tapping away on his phone. Amanda rose to her feet and straightened her jacket "It is likely that that the CPS are looking to proceed with the case against Ricky given that a barrister has been retained."

Phil looked up from his screen and dived straight in "we need to get on the offensive. We know that they are looking to try and make a case stick against you and I reckon we meet them head on with a big fuck you and we tell 'em to bring it on."

Amanda was taken aback by the reaction to this crudely blunt approach. "Yeah fuck it," erupted Ricky. He shot to his feet and grabbed Stephen's hair and gave it an enthusiastic pull "If they want a fight, I'll fucking fight them," he roared. He then gave a lighting quick demonstration of how quick he could throw punches as he showed off a combination or two. That's how you shadow box thought Amanda not the pathetic effort that she had been unlucky to see earlier from her roommate at Chambers. However, the memory that stayed with her for far longer though was that of how quickly Ryan seemed to go from a mild and placid young man to a veteran brawler. If this went to a trial, she was somehow going to have to keep the fighting hair-trigger reaction of her client out of the court room.

Stephen didn't enjoy his hair being yanked but Ricky was pumped up and knew he would never desert him. Never. He rose to his feet but not as vehemently, and he went in for a bear hug but the two men ended up stood shoulder to shoulder with their hands clasped either side of each other's head screaming into each other's faces "Fuck it," "FUCK IT," "FFFUUUUUUUUUUCCCCCCCKKKKKKK IIIIIIIITTTTTTT!!"

There was now far too much testosterone in the room for Amanda's liking especially as Phil was now joining in to make it a three way "fuck it," shouting match. She collected her notebook and pen and moved the solitary chair to the corner of the room and by the time she had done that the men had stopped their screeching and Phil was telling Ricky to get down to the police station with him. "What do you think?" Ricky asked of Amanda. "If we are looking at a fight then it might be the case that voluntarily attending the police station may have some future benefit but …," Phil cut off Amanda before she could finish advising her client. "Come on let's get on with it – fuck it," he roared as if he were a military commander like Lord Cardigan at the Charge of the Light Brigade.

The three men headed for the door under the direction of Phil and Amanda had no choice but to go with them as the alternative was an empty hotel room. She was anxious about what lay ahead and waiting outside the lift to take them back to the exit and the teeming streets of the metropolis the euphoria of a few moments before had worn off and there was a danger that someone was going to have a change of heart. Desperate to be the Alpha of the group, Phil decided he needed to try to keep encouraging Ricky and Stephen that his plan was the answer and in the next hour or so they'd be able to have a clean and straight fight if they wanted one.

Amanda hastily shuffled her mirror polished black shoes from side-to-side at least half a dozen times as they waited for the elevator and in doing so, she felt her lucky ankle bracelet bounce up and down on her left leg. It was a random thing to wear she appreciated that, but it began as a solution to a nervous trait which had developed without warning as she finished her final year at Oxford University. Back then and when Amanda was nervous or slightly uneasy, she would involuntarily lift her left leg off the floor. It even happened when she was sat down, and it was a most bizarre characteristic for a barrister to possess given the professional requirement to advocate in a court of law. However, and for reasons unbeknown to her there it was again as Amanda realised that she was not in actual fact shuffling her feet but the rocking motion was because her left foot wanted to come off the ground. She hoped no-one would notice and thankfully the lift appeared and chimed its arrival so when the doors opened to a dimly lit glass casket she was able to tap her right ankle against her left to feel that the ankle bracelet was in place as the three men were distracted in entering the elevator cabin.

The ten second journey down was not worth the minute wait. The passengers travelled in silence and the only sound to be heard was the screeching of the pulleys of a lift that was in desperate need of maintenance.

As soon as Amanda noticed her twitch and touched her lucky bracelet with her other leg the rising of the left foot seemed to dissipate. She was in no way an expert on anything medical, although the job had taught her a little, but her Aunt commented that she felt it maybe psychosomatic. The conclusion adopted was to wear an ankle bracelet to try and weight down her leg which was a preposterous, stupid idea but there it was and there it would stay and when, even for a brief moment, her left leg would inexplicably begin to rise touching her ankle bracelet would cause it to return to the floor.

This irrational set of memories and recollections had caused Amanda to blindly follow Phil, Stephen and Ricky out of the hotel and commence the walk to Charing Cross Police Station. This walk naturally took them in the direction of the scene of Saturday's events; a pub on the corner of Garrick Street and New Row. Ricky blanked it as they headed towards their destination down Bedford Street then a right turn onto Chandos Place then an almost immediate left onto Agar Street. Stephen shook his head as if the inanimate edifice was to blame for their collective current predicament. The only words came from Phil who spoke over his shoulder in Amanda's general direction to say "That's the pub."

Amanda only just caught those words over the typical cacophony in central London and she was mightily glad she did as it gave her the first sight of the pub that she had heard so much about of late. It didn't look too bad a place for a drink, not that Amanda would frequent such an establishment – "Lord No! Let's go to Dirty Martini," a cocktail bar on Covent Garden's Piazza "instead of here," she would have said if someone had suggested that they venture inside. As the distinctly unmerry band of four walked away Amanda slowed slightly just to make sure that her alert and retentive brain could scan as much of the surroundings as she could. One main entrance, glass from head to toe all the way around and what looked like a side door she thought she spotted as her neck craned back. The upstairs did not look like part of the pub but it was a massive building and this stayed in her head but walking down the incline of Bedford Street the final image was that of the large bay window that seemed to offer such a clear vantage point over the colonnade of the pedestrianised walkway below.

***

"For the benefit of the tape please confirm your name."

Ricky looked at Phil who sat with him pressed up against the inadequately sized table in interview room 'C' at Charing Cross Police Station. Phil nodded and Ricky gave his name.

"For the benefit of the tape please confirm your address." Ricky sought Phil's agreement once more and it was again given.

The interview had been going for about ten minutes. These things never move quickly, and Phil and Ricky were both getting restless. The police on the other side of the table had been ponderously slow in issuing the necessary formal caution to Ricky and explaining his rights under The Police and Criminal Evidence Act 1984.

Amanda had carefully counselled both Phil and Ricky in the foyer of the police station that the reason voluntary interviews were more common than they once were was because of budgetary cuts as formal ones that resulted in arrest and detention were too expensive. So a voluntary one meant that any prosecution steps could be balanced against the force's budget. Amanda's advice was right and she stressed the need for her to be in the room but Phil had previously cornered Ricky and had told him "This is what I do – this is my court room, hold Amanda back for another day."

Ricky, feeling overly pressurised, opted for Phil to go in with him. Stephen had of course offered but everyone including him knew full well that it was a kind but pointless gesture. Amanda, as ever the professional, smiled and accepted her exclusion with good grace however as the two men departed into the bowels of the station she was sure she caught sight of Phil giving her a smug 'he chose me' look. She could not be totally certain though but one thing for sure was that Amanda had not warmed to Phil at all.

Stephen paced up and down the waiting area of the police station for he could not sit still. Every time he got to either wall he'd turn and check his phone for the time. He did not want to talk either and other than Amanda offering the absolutely appropriate advice of "Phil is a trained police station advisor and he knows what he is doing," there was nothing else to say. She deliberately did not refer to him as a lawyer not just because that was the accurate description and for Stephen he would not have appreciated the distinction but Amanda did not want to give him the credit of a title he did not deserve. There was nothing to be gained though by publicly disparaging him so she continued with "and so Ricky is in the best of care for now and you and I need to try and just wait it out." Amanda doubted that Phil would have the politeness to refer to her in such professional terms.

After far too long for Amanda's liking, which she knew all too well meant further bad news and Stephen having done a marvellous job in getting his steps up for the day the security doors buzzed opened and into the foyer walked Phil with a face like thunder. Ricky sloped in behind him ashen faced and looking more than a little perturbed.

"What is it?" demanded Stephen even before the men were close enough to greet each other.

"Not here," snapped back Phil as he kept on walking out of the station and onto Agar Street. Ricky now with head down dragged his feet in the direction of Phil's hasty exit. Stephen followed and Amanda brought up the rear having thanked the desk clerk and checking under the immoveable chairs to make sure that nothing had been left behind.

Outside the afternoon sunshine hit against the paths and the reflection in the cream coloured concrete slabs almost made them appear golden. The streets of London were not actually paved with gold though and there was nothing treasurable about the outcome of the police interview. It was not lost on Ricky or Stephen that they were back outside the police station again but this time they'd swapped two of their band mates.

Phil did not wait to be asked he just launched straight in "Charged with GBH with intent and bailed to appear before magistrates tomorrow."

"What?" stammered back Stephen "I mean what the fuck … that quick … what's going on?"

Phil, stomping his feet in complete anger, spat out "That witness statement, they have names Ricky as throwing the punch that hit the guy."

The four were circling like native Americans around wagons as there was too much angst coursing through their bodies to stand still. Amanda's left foot was now completely off the floor to the point where she had no choice but to stand still and lean against a parking meter to steady herself.

"What witness … who … what?" Stephen spoke confused and more than a little out of his depth.

Amanda took control.

By placing her left index finger and thumb into a ring shape and placing into her mouth she let out a whistle that would have stopped an elephant in its tracks let alone a black cab. Amanda probably stopped a dozen or so taxis on the Strand a few hundred metres away as well but one was they all needed. On the apex of Agar Street and Chandos Place a carriage awaited them. No one even thought of asking where they were heading, they were just delighted to be going anywhere.

They piled in and sat wherever; no one was fussed in which direction they were facing. Amanda politely asked the driver to take them to Hartington Chambers Lincoln's Inn Fields. "Very nice," came the reply and the black cab headed off down Chandos Place towards the turning around Trafalgar Square and then slingshotting onto the Strand and then up Kingsway towards their destination.

The journey passed in silence. The cabbie sensing the atmosphere said nothing and just focused on his part of the transaction. Traffic for that part of the capital was not too bad and the journey took less than ten minutes but no one really enjoyed the sights of London as they passed them like Nelson's Column, The Savoy Hotel or a homeless man urinating in a bin.

The meter ticked over to 16:40 as the engine stopped outside the steps leading to the doors of Hartington Chambers. Amanda remembered the year 1640 as being the year that the first official slave was declared in the English colonies. Heaven knows how she knew that nor how she was able to recall it but that was Amanda's incredible retentive memory.

Thrusting the heavy car doors open everyone managed to exit the cab as elegantly as can really be done from such a vehicle. Amanda was last out and she had already fished out the synthetic feel twenty-pound note and paid it through the hatch with a cheery

"Thank you, keep the change."

"Cheers darlin," was the contented response and even before the four had passed under the Hartington Arch the cab was back off with light on and looking for its next fare.

Amanda was firmly in charge now. Phil grunted an almost inaudible thanks in respect of her paying for the cab. Amanda had not bothered to ask for a receipt as for her it was more important that the team got back on track than her trying to claim back a few pounds.

Into Chambers she led them and sticking her head into the clerks' room she saw a frantic looking scene, which to be fair was not an uncommon sight but there certainly seemed a different atmosphere than usual. Jimmy gave her a most bizarre look and when she asked for any available conference room, he was all but mute. Amanda didn't wait for permission, a most unlike her reaction, as she just led the three men, who were by now looking around in a little more awe of their surroundings than their taxi ride a few minutes before, off in search of an empty room.

As Amanda marched them through the narrow corridors towards one of the more remote meeting rooms she caught the eye of a few other members of Chambers and they all nodded and smiled in a way that they seemed to infer a degree of knowledge about something that she should also know.

Settling everyone into the comfy surroundings of a room that was far bigger and more resplendent that Ricky and Stephen's hotel room Amanda organised bottles of mineral water and little packets of biscuits. These boys must have been hungry as the snacks were devoured like human versions of the Cookie Monster from Sesame Street. She popped outside without being noticed during this feeding frenzy and went into two adjacent rooms and grabbed their bowls of biscuits and bottles of water and returned with arms laden full. All three men looked up and their crumb covered mouths smiled their satisfaction.

Amanda then began to talk. Phil was far less bullish now; he was not contrite at all but even his arrogance could not cover up the rather large bombshell that had been dropped. As ever the diplomat the words that were spoken did not seek to assert any blame or any hint of 'I told you so'.

"We know what case we need to defend now, and we know that the police and the CPS are pushing forward. We build Ricky's defence to the charge based on that there is only one person who actually saw Ricky throw the punch."

"But I didn't hit him," jumped in Ricky

"I understand that," assured Amanda "but we need to review the evidence that they allegedly have." Amanda refused the urge to use air quotes when saying the word allegedly.

"We are getting their file and evidence later this afternoon," confirmed Phil.

Ricky was feeling out of his depth and his head was spinning from the shock of the earlier interview.

Stephen, water bottle in hand, sent an update message to Ethan Harris. The text had been read but no immediate reply had been received.

Phil then declared, almost triumphantly, as he stared at his mobile phone that he had received an email from Trevor which copied in Lorna Williams at the CPS. Reaching for yet another packet of biscuits and not having his computer with him Amanda produced her laptop from her Mulberry bag and she inputted the password, which was the same one for all her accounts, Rump@le1. Phil was then able to forward his email onto her so they could immediately dissect what evidence the other side were going to rely on. Curiously when Amanda received the forwarded email, she noted that it had not been sent to her as well as Phil.

One attachment was an MP4 file containing a video clip from the CCTV cameras. The other attachment was the police file, such as it was, which included some very brief statements from the accused and one of the bar staff from The Circle House pub.

The CCTV footage was from various angles of that triangular intersection of Garrick Street, New Road and Bedford Street. The video was opened first. Phil was overly buoyant as it showed a melee, but no one seemed to throw a punch.

They watched it again and again.

They then watched it for a fourth time.

Stephen spoke first.

"Now you two," he was looking at Amanda and Phil as he spoke "are far cleverer than little old me but if there is no video of Ricky having punched anyone then it comes down to our word against theirs right?"

Amanda was actually impressed with the speed of Phil's response "It is not as simple as that I am afraid Stephen because…"

"But I didn't hit anyone," interjected Ricky.

"Sorry mate," replied Stephen "allegedly punched," and to Amanda's annoyance he used air quotes. "But here is my point if some guy got hurt then why does it have to be Ricky …" with a pause for some more water he concluded his sentence with "maybe I could say it was me?"

With that Amanda recoiled as if someone had

blown cigarette smoke in her direction.

Phil laughed.

"I don't think that we should talk about that," he calmly advised.

"Why?" asked Stephen "I am just thinking that Ricky's career is proper fucked if he goes down for this so why can't I put myself in the firing line." It was a lovely sentiment and Ricky turned to his trainer, manager and friend and smiled at him with a nod of deep gratitude for what Stephen was offering to do for him.

Amanda turned to her notes made from the earlier conversation and flicking through the reams of pages she found what she was looking for.

She read from her notepad "Cherry red chino trousers, white trainers, blue Hawaiian shirt with pineapple design."

"What?" was the almost unison response from Phil and Stephen. Ricky had still not said anything but was doing a tremendous job of scoffing his bodyweight in biscuits.

Amanda repeated what she had just read out and then she clicked play on the CCTV footage for a further time, and then only after a few seconds, she pressed pause to reveal a relatively clear image of someone at the edge of the ruckus facing the opposite direction to the camera but wearing white shoes, dark trousers and a light coloured patterned top. Amanda used the enlarge function on her computer to focus in on the design of the shirt and although it was pixelated the image was more like a pineapple than not.

"Yeah but what does that prove as the bloke is not outside yet?"

"What did you just say?" leapt in Amanda.

"Well as we both said earlier when it all kicked off it was chucking out time."

"Yes, yes I've got that," Amanda was feeling very impatient and said, "Go on," in a little too much of a school-teacher kind of way.

Stephen took the hint to get to the point "Well by the time the Peelers arrived on the scene the guy was out on the pavement." He pressed the screen on Amanda's laptop to where he recollected that the man ended up lying prostrate when the emergency services arrived. At the time the video clip was paused that man was not in the frame.

"So, who is to say that I didn't go back inside chin the bloke and then hey presto I'm in for a stretch?"

Phil commented quite correctly that that was unlikely given that the pub was closing, and Ricky was clearly in shot outside. "Yeah but what about ..." Stephen went on but Amanda was deep in thought and did not hear the rest of the conversation as she was asking herself an internal question; If the CCTV footage does not show the victim outside then where is the *actus reus*?

Actus reus is a Latin phrase that means 'guilty act' which is the physical component of a criminal act – in this case a punch.

Stephen and Phil's conversation was cut short and Amanda's thinking process was interrupted by a hefty knock knock and the face of Dave appearing around the door as it was inched open.

Silence engulfed the room.

"Sorry to interrupt but Miss may I have an urgent word?"

Dave rarely used the word urgent so Amanda knew straight away that she needed to step outside and judging from the serious look on Dave's face she didn't even have the time to finish the note she was half way through writing. "Apologies all I won't be long."

The door had not even closed when Dave was ushering Amanda through another and into an empty room. He made sure the door was firmly shut before he started speaking but the first thing he said was "I'm bloody starving and there are no pissing biscuits in this room!" Under normal circumstances Amanda would have confessed to having pilfered them but she was far more interested in knowing what was so urgent rather than sating the clerk's appetite.

Dave opened a few drawers and chuntered a few further expletives as he did not find what he was hunting for.

"Dave what on earth is going on? I saw a couple of colleagues not that long ago and they were also behaving slightly strangely too."

"Amanda," her name being spoken to her face by Dave made her left foot come up almost to the height of her right knee. She fell into a chair.

Dave continued with a look of immense pain on his face as if he were telling her that something had happened to her Aunt or Uncle.

"I know who opposing Counsel is on the O'Ryan matter."

"Jesus Dave," exclaimed Amanda with utter relief as she let out the breath that she had been holding in for too long.

"Who is it then?" asked Amanda with a little too much insistence in her tone.

Dave looked down and said nothing immediately.

"Tell me Dave!" she demanded. He could only mutter "It's someone in Chambers."

Amanda's pupils darted around her eyes like fireflies caught in a jam jar.

"Rufus?" she asked raising her eyebrows

Dave shook his head glumly.

Amanda's eyebrows then shot up almost to her hair line as she bounced to her feet. The dots were joined in her head and she just shook her head in disbelief.

"Trevor?"

Dave nodded.

"Well that explains the shadow boxing then."

"What?" it was now Dave's turn to look bewildered.

"Doesn't matter." Amanda said dismissively and followed on with "Chinese walls it is then Dave."

Dave nodded again. "We will make sure that any information is subject to strict disclosure and that you are both, temporarily, not roommates." He added that he would clerk for her and that Jimmy would do likewise for Trevor. He then made a terrible effort at being funny by apologising for Amanda landing the wooden spoon. It was not the time for levity.

Amanda was about to speak when Dave continued "Rufus has called all of Chambers together in the main lobby to make an announcement."

"What now?" she enquired

"Yes Miss," said Dave then he added "Now."

Amanda went for the brass door handle and Dave put his hand on hers.

"Amanda," he looked straight into her green eyes "I am sorry, but I only just found out myself."

She smiled back "One of those things Dave. Let me just tell my clients that I need fifteen minutes or so." It was Dave's turn to smile.

Having updated the three men, but without telling them all of the information she now knew, Dave and

Amanda marched back towards Chambers' lobby.

As they walked, she asked the question that was in the forefront of her mind "So Dave how did this happen?"

Dave sighed "When I was out Jimmy took a call and placed the prosecution brief with Mr Houghton-Hamper and had the paperwork all done and dusted before I got back."

"Well done him," Amanda spoke with a little too much sarcasm.

"Not ideal for sure," came back. Then he asked the question that was top of his list "You could always consider declining to act further?"

There was never any way Amanda was going to do that and the clerk knew it, but he felt he should raise it.

"No chance! Trevor should do it if anyone does," said Amanda but they both knew that with his comparatively insignificant case load there was no prospect of him turning down a case as by doing so he could well end up being black-listed by the CPS for any future work. There was no way he would do that, not even for Amanda.

The two arrived to find the entirety of Chambers gathered together in a huddle in the central area of the lobby. There were so many people there, from clerks to other Queen's Counsel and members of Chambers, support staff and accounts team. Dave was looking around to see if the sodding night-time cleaners had been called in for this as well. Trevor was nowhere to be seen but given that he was not gifted with great height either that was perhaps no surprise.

As Amanda and Dave were noticed by the expectant throng as having arrived the mass of bodies parted like the Red Sea to make an even sided channel following the marble flooring from Amanda's shoes all the way down to a jubilant looking Rufus Hetherington-Jones.

With a gesture to the late comers through a tap of his watch he began to address the group before him. "Now that we are all present, I would like a few moments of your precious and collective time." Most people silently groaned as with this type of introduction there was little doubt that Rufus was unbearably going to exact as much attention for himself as possible and of course the irony being, that by saying he only wanted a few moments of their precious time, he was actually taking up more of it.

"Today is a first for Hartington Chambers as two of our illustrious juniors take up the noble advocacy battle that we are all so passionate about, but this time on opposing sides." The use of the term junior was rather inappropriate. It was Rufus' way of reminding everyone that he was Queen's Counsel and his name was engraved on Chambers' archway only a few feet from where he was standing. Also this news was not breaking as it had been around Chambers for at least an hour or two before Rufus convened this get together but still people deferred to their notional boss and allowed him to remain centre stage and the purveyor of 'new' information.

"Our Trevor Hamper-Houghton is for the Crown," he began a steady clap which eventually found company as Trevor emerged from a dense group of listeners. Then rather amazingly he went up to the Head of Chambers, as if it were school awards day, and shook his hand.

Rufus enjoyed this moment, but few others did.

"And then for the Defence we have the rather

lovely Amanda Buckingham." There was no need whatsoever for the 'rather lovely' and every woman, including Amanda and indeed some of the male attendees as well, winced with embarrassment and discomfort. Eyes turned to Amanda and the clerks made a clamour of cheers and foot stamping that droned out the polite and respectful clapping that had been afforded to Trevor.

Amanda stood, a picture of professional calmness, as she raised her left hand in a semi-salute to Rufus who simply nodded in return.

As the lobby returned to near silence Rufus raised both arms for complete quiet. He then incredulously explained to one and all that he had selflessly taken on a new instruction which enabled Amanda to be made available to accept this particular case. On hearing this Amanda's left leg wanted to rise up, not in anxiety but in rage, and kick her Head of Chambers squarely between the legs. She resisted the temptation of course but it did not stop her thinking about doing it. Dave looked down at his feet in order that his shock was not visible at this complete fib.

Rufus then went on to explain how he had also been instrumental in placing the CPS in the capable hands of Trevor which in itself was a hefty leap in the direction of inaccuracy. Jimmy didn't mind really as he was just pleased to have placed his first brief.

"So that I suppose this all makes me a boxing promoter." No one laughed other than Rufus. He pressed on unaware that he was the only one enjoying his oratory skills "So now that we have met the competitors we wish there to be a fair fight with no low blows, and when one stands victorious over the other at the end of the final round, that in actual fact the real winners of this gladiatorial contest will be Justice and Hartington Chambers!"

Rufus, if truth be told, did not know a great deal about boxing at all but he hoped that the occasional pun would have got a laugh or at least a grin from one or two present but he was not that lucky. He had a smile from Dave but that was about it and despite Rufus' desperation to be the wittiest person in the room he would only ever achieve that accolade if he was stood alone. As for what he had hoped to be a rousing speech met with cheering and calls for quiet he was even unluckier. His reference to Hartington Chambers at the end was greeted with a handful of nods but not the wild adulation he had hoped for.

He gave it one more try.

"So with the first round tomorrow it's seconds out and good luck to both."

Sensing that blissfully this was the end, Rufus received a decent volume of applause that he revelled in but actually the clapping was more because it had ended rather than for the quality of the words spoken or how they were delivered.

Amanda did not wait around as she rushed back to the three men and her conference.

Trevor and Rufus were the last to leave the lobby, enjoying a few undeserved pats on the back. One senior member of Chambers offered to place a little wager on Trevor being victorious, which made Rufus think of perhaps running a book on the outcome, but he was not really very cognisant of odds, stakes and other betting terminology either so he laughed it off. However when he reflected later that day it occurred to him that maybe a discreet wager, for a bottle of Fonseca Vintage Port, would appeal to him far more than having to sully himself by running a gambling book with all that uncivilised handling of money.

Dave had been collared by at least three other barristers asking how they had not been consulted about the case given their extensive experience. Dave replied saying that Amanda had been asked for specifically, so his hands were tied. They accepted his entirely bogus answer with professional bad grace and a great deal of chuntering as they meandered away to find something else to complain about.

Amanda was alone in the corridor and she was inwardly furious. 'Really lovely' how dare he! She reached the door to the meeting room and taking a moment to compose her mind she walked straight in to find the three men chatting about who deserved the final pack of biscuits.

"Good you're back," went in Phil "So Ricky thinks that he is due the…"

"It's Trevor Hamper-Houghton," interrupted Amanda.

That stopped Phil mid-sentence.

Ricky spoke, which pleased Amanda to know he had not lost the power of speech "Who is this Trevor Hughton Hampden bloke?"

"Trevor Hamper-Houghton is a member of these Chambers explained Amanda and she waved her arms around the room as she expressed the words "these Chambers."

"Does that matter?" came in Stephen.

Phil, and again to his credit, took that one for Amanda "No not all; it's no different to two boxers from the same stable fighting each other." That resonated well with Ricky and Stephen and their momentary scepticism disappeared as quickly as the final packet of biscuits did into Ricky's stomach. It did not matter that Phil's answer was complete bullshit and both he and Amanda knew it.

Albeit a first for Hartington Chambers it was not that uncommon for opposing Counsel to come from the same set, but it certainly could cause issues over access to clerks, resources and potentially raise concerns over the accidental disclosure of confidential or case sensitive information.

Amanda nodded and smiled at Phil and he tried to smile back but his face had clearly been out of practice and he offered more of a 'show me your teeth' expression but it was the most favourable interaction they'd had all day.

Judging the mood of the room she headed off the issue of the CPS instructing Trevor, with a simple statement that was greeted with the same reaction as if she had announced she had just secured Ricky a multi-fight contract with Golden Boy Promotions worth a billion US Dollars. "I've never lost a case and I don't intend to start now. I know Trevor very well and he will stick to what he does best which is to keep to the technicalities of the process whereas we will defend this on proving beyond reasonable doubt that someone else threw the punch."

Amanda then added the comment which caused fists to be banged against the crumb covered mahogany table. She wanted to add that she had no intention of losing to Trevor, but she opted for the far more unifying remark of "We will not lose this case!"

"Fuck yeah," screamed Stephen and he grabbed Rick's head and gave it a shake. "Get off," was Ricky's only reply. Phil went for his phone and started issuing commands almost immediately, Amanda doubted the recipient had even heard their ring before the orders came tumbling down the line. He was clearly instructing Kelly King on the arrangements for tomorrow's Magistrates Hearing.

The confidence in the room was infectious and Amanda was penning down some possible opening remarks, just in case any were needed, at Court tomorrow. Sometimes the Magistrate would seek more than just an immediate transfer up to the Crown Court and if it was going to be one of those days she wanted to be as best prepared as possible.

Looking down at the notes she had written just before Dave had called her to Rufus' announcement, two letters 'CC' stood out which to Amanda meant Crown Court.

Phil was off the phone and with perhaps a little causality he proposed a shopping trip to T.M. Lewin on Southampton Row which was only a handful of minutes' walk away. "Why?" asked Ricky. "You are not going near a courtroom looking and smelling like that so it's a fresh outfit from top to bottom." Stephen shuffled in his chair and Phil correctly identified why "It's on us," as he waved a corporate credit card in the direction of the two men. Stephen stammered over his reply of "hey nice one," as he tried to be relaxed about not needing to find money for new clothes.

"I am going to take these two straight to the clothes shop and then back to the hotel for a quiet night before the hearing tomorrow." Phil stated and then in a team focused way asked, "Is that alright with you Amanda?"

"Of course, and we will meet here at Chambers at 09:30."

That would normally have been the end of the conference, but Ricky had something to ask that he had been literally dying to get off his chest. "What do I do?"

Phil didn't wait "Do nothing unless asked and if you are just say not fucking guilty and fuck all else."

Amanda would not have directly indicated to any of her clients how they should plead but it wouldn't have been a good end to a productive meeting if she had rebuked Phil. So she elected for a witty comment in reply. "If you are asked, which you may not be of course, I'd probably miss out the 'fucking' if I were you."

Everyone laughed.

She said her goodbyes for now to the three men who departed down the steps of Chambers' entrance to more than enough peering eyes but either they didn't notice, or they didn't care. Amanda wished that she was not so self-conscious most of the time.

Amanda was overburdened with bags, notepads and textbooks so she kicked her door to open it but all that happened was that she stumbled back as she lost her balance. Books were dropped and paperwork too, for the door had been locked from the inside.

Trevor's face stuck itself around the now unlocked and open door. "Oh, it's you." He didn't offer to help Amanda pick up the various items that were strewn over the floor. He actually stepped back so he spoke through the tiniest of cracks "I can't help you in case I see something that I should not."

No, you just don't want to was what Amanda thought of saying but instead she said nothing except "Are you going to let me in?"

Trevor fumbled over his reply as if he had been caught with a woman in his bedroom by his overly regimented father.

"Look I just need a few bits from my desk and then

our room is yours for now." Amanda stressed the words our and for now.

Trevor opened the entrance with such an elaborate swing and wave of his hand he could have easily been a Master of Ceremonies at a circus introducing 'The Great Bambilino' or some other headline act.

"Thank you," said Amanda as she regained access to her shared space. Looking around the floor she located an old set of papers that had been boxed up and were awaiting return to that particular firm of instructing solicitors. She carefully took out the documents and made a pile on the edge of her desk and she began to fill the now empty container with various items that she thought she might need if further entry to the room was going to be restricted. In went highlighters, pens, post it notes of all shapes, sizes and one colour; hot pink, a phone charger, her lap top charger, three USB sticks and on top of that assorted collection of hefty stationary, went the bundle of papers that moments before she had been picking off the carpet outside.

Looking around and deciding that with her bag on top of the box she was not going to be able to take much more she would have said a pleasant farewell, but off went her phone. Delving into her bag she caught the dialler just before it went to voicemail. It was a mobile number she did not have saved to her contacts.

"Hello Amanda Buckingham speaking."

"It's Phil," she heard.

"Wait one second," she marched out of the room and closed the door behind her. "Everything okay?" she hesitantly asked.

"Oh yeah all good," came back the breezy reply "They are back in their hotel room and Ricky looks like a cheap estate agent but is happy enough. I just wanted to ask if you fancied a quick drink before I head back to the station."

Was this the same Phil? Amanda, puzzled by this nice but slightly odd offer, replied the only way she should "I'd have loved to but its prep for me tonight as I want to review the evidence we've received and take a look through my notes as well. But when we win this thing we will go for a drink or three."

"Deal." Phil replied. Then he hung up.

Smiling to herself she opened the door and walked straight in.

Trevor jumped like a cat being squirted with a water pistol.

Amanda stood rooted to the spot with a face completely full of amazement.

"Trevor, what were you just doing?"

"Nothing I mean obviously something you know I was standing here of course and er … I was er … worried that …" He didn't know what to say so Amanda asked him the direct question as her shoulder bag that was placed on top of the box's contents was now back on her desk. "Were you just looking at my notes?"

"Absolutely no way, actually how dare you accuse me of such things and actually that is a matter that I have a good mind to report you for to The Bar Council." Trevor felt the best policy here was to go on the offensive.

He was wrong.

"Trevor of all people …" Amanda might as well have severed his femoral artery with how those four words were delivered. She replaced her bag on the top of the box and picking it up she went for the door.

Trevor said nothing but opened it up for her and as they passed each other Amanda shook her head in bitter disappointment and kept on walking. Trevor was cross with himself, but he was cross with himself for getting caught not for this actions.

Travelling home she was so disillusioned by what she might have caught Trevor doing. She replayed the events over and over again and despite her near photographic memory Amanda was not totally certain as she fished the ringing phone out of her bag that she hadn't put it on the table rather than back in the box.

Her night did not go to plan. She fed a grateful Rumpole and gave him some much-needed attention before the prep work for the hearing tomorrow could start. She was still feeling disconsolate, so she ordered her usual take-away but this time, and for the first time as well, they forgot the extra pineapple on her thin and crispy Hawaiian pizza. Amanda then dropped a glass of fresh orange juice on her Louis De Poortere Hadschlu rug and the next hour or so was spent trying to tidy that mess up.

Hunched over the ever-worsening stain she gave up and rocked back on her heels and for only the second time that year she had a cry. It had been a really trying couple of days and she was not sure whether it was spilling the last of the orange juice on a very expensive Persian rug or the lack of extra pineapple that made her shed a few tears.

Now feeling a little cross she stood up and threw the soaking wet tea towel onto the floor and stomped off to bed but with a firm resolve to wake early and prep like she had never prepped before.

Her last thought before she fell asleep was "How could they forget extra pineapple?"

An hour later she was awake and alert. Pineapple she cried out loud as she jumped out of bed. In doing so she scared Rumpole, who was sleeping next to her, so much that he may well have lost one of his nine lives.

Amanda tipped the entire contents of the box she had packed up from her desk and office onto her antique French bureau and sweeping away all the stationary she poured into her notepad. CC, she found written on her notepad but she had surmised earlier that it was a reference to Crown Court but it wasn't at all.

Pulling open her laptop with the elegance and patience of a child opening presents on their birthday she found the email from Phil that showed the footage they had watched and discussed earlier. The letters CC she wrote down earlier would have been finished with a further two consonants to make CCTV if she had not been entirely sidetracked by Dave's urgent interruption.

The night for that area of London was surprisingly quiet and yet the internal cogs of Amanda's brain were making a tremendous racket as they worked overtime to cope with the speed of her thoughts.

She must have watched the footage a dozen times and at each time when it came to its abrupt end the words of Stephen rang in her ears like World War Two air raid sirens.

He had said "the bloke is not outside yet," so where is the next few seconds of the CCTV footage. Could it be possible that Trevor had not only been snooping through her notes, even for just a fraction of time, and that he or the CPS had also not disclosed the entire recording?

This time Amanda, even though she was tired and needed sleep, forced herself to write out full notes so nothing was overlooked in a few hours' time.

Back to bed she went and Rumpole snuggled up to her and gave off a set of deep and melodic purrs that sent her off to sleep without another thought of pineapple.

Amanda arrived at Chambers early and was ready, notes in hand to greet a rather dapper looking Ricky. She knew what Phil had meant about the estate agent look for the suit was cut to the super thin style and had more than a glint of shine about it but nevertheless he looked smart. Stephen was dressed in a new shirt and tie and even though both men clearly did not know their way around an iron at least effort had been made. Phil wore yet another three-piece suit combination and he looked every part the typical criminal law case officer.

As this gang of four headed towards their pre-booked room Trevor Hamper-Houghton appeared. Was it a coincidence or not? Amanda wasn't sure. As they passed each other there was definitely an element of hostility between them, added to in no small way as Amanda shook her head disapprovingly at him and they walked on by without a word being spoken.

Trevor was off for his meeting with Lorna Williams of the CPS.

Whilst both meetings were taking place inside Hartington's offices, Dave and Jimmy had arranged for them to be separated at either ends of Chambers' extensive premises. Trevor was standing in the bay window of his meeting room looking out onto the concrete quadrangle beneath him, trying to adopt a John F. Kennedy style pose as if he and the late great

President of the United States of America shared similar intellectual and emotional burdens. There was a polite knock at the door and as he called out "Enter" he was delighted to see Lorna. Her hair was pulled back into a ponytail and she was wearing a very smart dark business suit with an open necked white shirt. He stepped forward to formally introduce himself, "It's wonderful to finally meet you" he opened with. Her reaction pleased him greatly "Yes indeed THH and it's good to put a face to the voice". Trevor went red as he brushed off his embarrassment with a waft of the papers he was holding in his right hand and a stuttering "Thank you thank you, please take a seat won't you?"

Their meeting was conducted in a very formal and professional manner with them both agreeing that the likely plea from the accused was going to be 'Not Guilty'. Trevor reassured Lorna that he would do everything in his power to ensure a conviction at the GBH with intent charge.

On a lower floor and the other side of Chambers, Amanda, Phil, Stephen and Ricky had a far less formal discussion. Amanda had ensured that there was more than enough of a stock of biscuits to be scoffed. They passed the time ensuring that Ricky was aware of what was going to happen and that he was as comfortable as he could possibly be.

As the clock ticked down to departure time, a silence began to creep into both rooms. It was not intentional on anyone's part, but it was perhaps more out of each and every person just naturally reflecting on their private thoughts as to how their day might play out.

As is often the case with initial hearings at Magistrates Court it was over before it really began.

Ricky stood in the dock looking nervous.

Amanda and Trevor momentarily debated one or two minor points and the Magistrates read out the charge and the injuries suffered which included a fractured jaw, two lost teeth and a bleeding nose. She decided to hold fire on the missing CCTV footage until the Plea and Trial Preparation Hearing which occurs at the Crown Court and is the precursor to the main trial. When she had carefully studied and concluded that the Magistrates were clearly not interested in doing anything other than moving this case up to the Crown Court as soon as they could in order to get it off their docket she refrained from making any arguments about the evidence. It could wait, and probably was better suited anyway, to the Plea and Trial Preparation Hearing she rationalised.

The anticipatory waiting around to be called in lasted far in excess of the hearing itself and Ricky, having been reminded of his caution and bail restrictions, found himself back in another taxi with his three team members before he really knew what had happened. He was the first one to speak as the vehicle sped away "So was that it then?"

Phil nodded.

"Oh," came back a rather jaded Ricky.

"So, what's next?" questioned Stephen.

Phil went to speak, but before he started, he caught a glimpse of Amanda's open mouth poised to respond. He deferred to the barrister with an apologetic wave of his right hand.

"Thanks Phil." Amanda smiled at Phil who tried to reciprocate but he had not got any better at smiling in the last twenty-four hours.

"You may have heard the Magistrates and I discuss

a Plea and Trial Preparation Hearing."

"Yeah," chorused Stephen and Ricky.

"Well rather surprisingly it has been listed for tomorrow. It is not normally that quick but actually it serves us well as we get to move forward and start preparing your detailed defence." Amanda added with a little more conviction "Also it means that the other side get less time to prepare their case and remember it is them that need to prove the charge."

She sounded confident but when the Magistrates decreed, of their own accord, the date of the next court appearance Amanda would have preferred more time but so be it. In her experience of handling cases in the lower court, arguing with those sitting behind the bench was never a wise course of action. The Magistrates decision to expedite Ricky's case had been based on a series of related actions involving shareholder fraud in a major investment house being suddenly adjourned as result of allegations of evidence tampering. Therefore, the sometimes interminable wait for court allocation was not going to be suffered on this case and Amanda opted for the positive spin rather than a negative one.

"There seems to be a fuck load of pointless toing and froing," declared Stephen.

It was Phil's turn to respond with "yeah."

Sensing that everyone could do with a few hours rest and recuperation, and Amanda included herself in that, they agreed to meet the next day for the initial Crown Court hearing. This was on the understanding that if anything was needed by anyone, they could call her at any time of the day. Amanda distributed her business cards to everyone even though Ricky now had three of them in his wallet.

There was preparatory work to be done and that

was the plan for the remainder of Amanda's day. Although she did find the time to manage the most urgent of her email inbox which, if it were an actual physical box, it would have been overflowing. However and despite a real but quite common peccadillo of wanting not to see the red circle with a white number in it indicating that something was unread she realised that, just this once, her email response rate would have to be slightly worse than immediate.

***

Thursday morning came around quicker than most were expecting. Ricky and Stephen were suffering from a severe case of cabin fever having been cooped up in a space that was too small to swing a London rat let alone a cat.

Phil and Amanda waited outside Chambers with a black cab already poised for the journey to Court. One stood looking towards the expected arrival point of Stephen and Ricky and the other was keeping a watchful eye on the ever-increasing meter.

Ricky and Stephen arrived only a few minutes behind their appointed arrival time and they all climbed into yet another taxi.

Today's trip to court was for the formal declaration of Ricky's plea. He knew, as did everyone else, that it was going to be a submission of 'Not Guilty' to the charge of Grievous Bodily Harm with intent to cause GBH.

As this was declared by Ricky in the dock later that morning there was not even a muttering of surprise from anyone present. Ricky then sat there for the next hour and a half listening to bewigged advocates debate the finer points of criminal trial preparation. He was lost by it all, only the occasional smile and mouthed words of "keep your chin up," from Stephen kept him from losing his mind and doing or saying something completely stupid. As Ricky was sat, his moment to speak two important words a long and distant memory, he received the third, or was it the fourth, version of "keep your chin up," from Stephen who was sat in the public gallery. It was an odd thing for him to mouth as when Ricky was in a different cornered off arena Stephen would bellow at him "Keep your chin down!" The inconsistency was not lost on either of them, but Stephen was doing his best in trying to keep Ricky's spirits up and even though it was never said, he did appreciate it.

Ricky had a prime seat to watch the technical debate between the barristers, but as he watched Amanda and Trevor argue over this and that, he couldn't help but wonder why Stephen, Michael and Connor had not been asked to give their version of events. The reason for this was that Stephen had that night declared himself "battered" so he wanted to go and get some greasy battered food. Connor and Michael were, and not for the first time that day, involved in a disagreement over a couple of girls which, even under times of no fiscal restraint, would the authorities have any interest in bringing before a court.

"If I could turn now to the evidence received thus far," lead Amanda. This statement was directed to Judge Emily Brannigan who was presiding over her umpteenth Crown Court matter of that year. Brannigan was not ferociously intelligent but ferocious and intelligent and if required she was not afraid to deploy either of those weapons at her disposal. The court clerks feared and respected her in equal measure, but they enjoyed the occasion every year when, on her birthday, Judge Brannigan would bring in homemade cheese scones and her now infamous lemon meringue pie. As for those that appeared before her, the barristers knew that ninety-nine per cent effort was nowhere near enough.

"Yes," said the Judge but it was not a positive stated affirmative it was more "if you must."

Amanda respectfully replied with a thank you, but she didn't say it with a great deal of sentiment. This tone resulted in a sharp look from Judge Brannigan.

"As we have discussed earlier those that instruct me," she was referring to Kelly King Solicitors "received an email with a copy of the relevant CCTV recording for the time in question."

"Yes," said the Judge with even less enthusiasm than before and a look that left it in no doubt that her patience was dwindling and rapidly.

The hearing was approaching its third hour and Amanda sensed quite correctly that there was a general malaise settling over the Court room and not just in the Judge's seat. This often occurs when hearings drag on for too long with no respite and no fresh air so she therefore did not coherently and eruditely set up the point in the way that the experienced advocate would have preferred.

"The CCTV footage does not indicate that there was any physical and or actionable conduct befitting of the charge before the Court today, and most certainly not involving the accused." Amanda pointed to Ricky in the dock as she addressed the Judge.

There was more than a murmur of approval from Stephen and Phil and these words finally woke Ricky from his mental stupor, and he began to turn his head frantically left to right and back again as if he were watching a remarkable tennis rally on Wimbledon's Centre Court, rather than his actual location of sitting in the dock at Nailton Crown Court.

Amanda stood behind the desk which was to the left hand side as the Judge viewed the Court room and she indicated by an outstretched hand that opposing Counsel needed to address a material and fundamental deficiency in the Crown's case against her client. After all there could be no GBH with intent conviction if there was no *actus reus* event.

Trevor was slow to react.

Amanda took the bait.

"My learned friend appears hesitant to respond." Even these words did not elicit much protest from Trevor so with confidence growing Amanda pressed on. "Which could infer that he is only too cognisant of the evidential uncertainty relating to the case for the Prosecution." She paused for breath and there was still nothing from her colleague at Hartington Chambers. "Therefore, and given that the fine members of the jury, yet to be sworn in, will be asked to decide this case beyond a reasonable doubt I suggest that the Court may wish to consider whether or not the case against my client should reasonably continue."

With that she sat down hearing whispered approving sounds of 'well done' and 'good job' from Phil behind her and a rather uncouth energetic round of applause from Stephen. This clapping was not well received by the Judge, who was a stickler for order and decorum in her court and she sent Stephen a look that turned his very core to ice; he never moved another inch until it was time to leave.

Judge Emily Brannigan was, in private, a fan of Amanda. Although they had nothing in common to unite them as she went to Jesus College Cambridge and Amanda studied at Lady Margaret Hall Oxford, they were members of different inns and didn't even share any of the same academic memberships. Nevertheless, Brannigan paid particular attention to the increasing meteoric rise of this barrister from Hartington Chambers and she was personally delighted in the way that Amanda took no prisoners and didn't shy away from confrontation. Brannigan realised why she had taken a special interest in Amanda; she reminded her of herself.

Trevor had still not done or said anything, and this began to discomfort Amanda ever so slightly. Surely not even Trevor could just hope that the Judge would overlook such a chasmic gap in the chain of causation between allegation and conviction.

The Judge addressed Amanda's unease with a professional but devastating comment.

"Counsel are you suggesting that there is no evidence of the elements of the charge levied against him." Brannigan didn't wait for Amanda's response despite the fact that one was ready, and she sprang to her feet like a startling cat. The Judge continued "I am dismayed and greatly concerned for the fair treatment of your client if that is the case as I have, on my screen, a tranche of the CCTV footage of the victim falling out onto the streets outside the public house." The Judge moved her head to the right and began to play the video clip showing the moments after the end of what Amanda had already seen and studied.

"Er … I have not seen that," spluttered Amanda. Her left leg spasmed.

Trevor did and said nothing.

"Excuse me Counsel are you indicating to the Court that you were not aware of the existence of CCTV footage?" asked Judge Brannigan.

"No I knew about the CCTV recording … What I meant to say is that … er … may I have a moment to confer with those instructing me please?"

The Judge, irritated and a little disappointed, scowled her approval and added "I suggest you take more than a moment Miss Buckingham." Suitably rebuked Amanda turned to face Phil who was frantically delving through his papers whilst at the same time searching for the email that he had received which contained the evidence.

He found it after a few seconds which, to him, felt like hours. Scrolling down as quick as his finger could drag the cursor, he shook his head to indicate he had nothing to add or say.

Amanda's heart was beating faster than Trevor's would have done after two cortado coffees in a day and her left foot was now fully off the floor to the point where she had to hold onto the edge of the table with her right hand.

"Take your time," was the heavily sarcastic comment from the judicial bench. Phil had gone red and was sweating profusely.

He looked at the email again and was frantically searching. Unlike the first time he searched he dragged the page on his computer screen to the very bottom where the email waivers and signatures often get collated together and there, not obvious at all, in the far right corner was another folder. It was buried between lines and lines of text about 'if you receive this email in error blah blah blah'.

Phil frantically clicked the file to open it, but he was only greeted with an error message saying that it was corrupted and was unable to be downloaded. Amanda, still standing, turned to the Judge and offered a contrite comment that the second video clip file had been located. She tried to justify the position adopted by explaining where the folder was found.

"I would have thought that rather than suggesting the prosecution's case lacked material evidence, you would have actually been able to verify if you had received all of the evidence rather than wasting all of our collective time," stated the Judge.

Amanda winced with professional discomfort.

Some barristers would use this chance to deflect any embarrassment away from themselves and pass it to their instructing solicitors who tended to occupy the rows of tables and chairs behind. Amanda was not that type of barrister.

"It would appear that a folder was provided but it is corrupted and therefore renders it incapable of being analysed and reviewed."

The Judge didn't wait for Amanda to finish her sentence.

"This appears to be a retraction Miss Buckingham, am I correct?"

There was nothing to say but, yes. She tried her best to conceal her affirmation though, "It may be the case that a folder was provided however the Defendant has been potentially prejudiced in not having the opportunity to …"

"I'll stop my learned friend there I think," pounced Trevor as he got to his feet with the speed of a passenger trying to be first at the exit doors after a plane had landed, "that is not what was offered to the

Court a few moments ago."

"Would you like the transcript of this hearing to be read back to you Miss Buckingham?" enquired the Judge.

Amanda's reply was courteous but laced with a hefty dose of acidity "No thank you and provided that a further version, but this time in a correct and readable format is provided immediately, I consider that too much of the Court's time has been allocated already to this specific point."

"I entirely agree," confirmed the Judge disdainfully and then she added, "Trial is listed for two days on the next available dates and given that there is clearly some degree of necessity to firmly manage the effective administration of this case I will reserve this matter to be tried by myself."

This was not a question from Judge Emily Brannigan but rather a statement however she received nods of agreement from both barristers.

The final words from the bench were saved for Trevor. "Mr Hamper-Houghton I trust the broken file was just one of those things."

"I apologise to the Court," he replied. Amanda noted that he didn't immediately offer any apology to her or Ricky but before she could make that point, he spoke further "and of course the Crown offers its apologies to my learned friend. It is of course regretful that one part of the CCTV footage was damaged however we would naturally have rectified this unintentional and accidental oversight, if the Crown had known in advance of today's court attendance that the Defence had not adequately received this part of the evidence."

"Indeed," was the only word spoken and that came

from Judge Brannigan as she rose. As is court protocol everyone else stood and nodded in the direction of the Royal Arms behind the judge's chair. All were just about in unison to adhere to this legal custom save for Ricky and Stephen who were a good five seconds behind.

Amanda wanted to scream at Trevor. He must have done that deliberately for certain. It was far too convenient that the email was not sent to her and the second video clip was damaged and hidden way down at the bottom of the email.

Instead of screaming at Trevor she smiled at him and said, "Well played," and she left, with Phil following hard on her heels, without another word.

"What a bastard!" exclaimed Phil once Ricky and Stephen had re-joined them. One had come from the dock and one from the gallery but following the look Stephen had received from Judge Brannigan, it was he who looked like he had the harder of the experiences.

The four were standing in one of the many passageways that made up the warren that is Nailton Crown Court.

"I'm sorry," Amanda squeezed Ricky's hand as she spoke to him. There was little physical affection reciprocated as he placed his other palm over her knuckles. His words were far warmer "It's absolutely fine. It's like a fight isn't it? You might not win every round but as long as you get the decision at the end, it doesn't matter."

"Well said mate," chipped in Stephen whose internal core was now returning back to normal temperature after its abrupt chilling earlier.

When they had all decamped back to Chambers the video file had already been sent over. Again, the email was only sent to Phil.

As they viewed the clip they could recognise Stephen by his dark trousers and inconspicuous shirt and he was holding what resembled a styrofoam take-away box which occasionally would be opened and its contents stuffed towards the general direction of his mouth. Connor and Michael were spotted as the throng seemed to suddenly disperse. Connor's dark hair and light jean jacket identified him as he approached Stephen in the footage and right behind him was Michael whose open sports jacket and cropped denim trousers were unmistakable.

The four continued to watch and then it happened.

Two women, clearly identifiable by long hair and the clothes they wore came into shot exiting the pub by a side security door. Almost immediately afterwards a man literally fell out of the pub through the door like he had been felled by a lumberjack, as he tumbled over and ended up laying sprawled on the concrete another man then stumbled into sight and he looked behind him as the door slammed closed. As a group of people rushed to the prone male the other man sauntered towards Stephen, Michael and Connor. It was so obviously Ricky, that when Stephen volunteered that fact Phil looked at him with amazement.

Moments later and after a lot of gesticulating from those in shot, two police officers arrived, and they clearly took charge of the situation promptly and effectively. One even pointed directly to the camera they were now watching the recording from. It was not that long until the officers took hold of Ricky and turned him around, so he too faced the camera as they placed the handcuffs on him.

"Okay," said Phil trying to be casual.

Amanda looked at Ricky and articulated what three of the four people present were thinking "Everything Ricky. I asked for everything."

"I didn't lie," pleaded the boxer.

"You have not been a fucking saint though have you?" hollered Phil.

***

Trevor was content with a good job done. He hung around the clerks' room and the lobby at Hartington Chambers making sure that anyone who looked remotely in his general direction got the full version of how well, in his humble opinion, he had performed.

Rufus tried to skip up the stone steps, but he was distracted by trying to catch yet another glimpse of his name carved into the archway. He stumbled into the lobby and was greeted by a smug looking Trevor.

"I heard you won the open round dear boy," enunciated the Head of Chambers who was slightly out of breath.

"It was more like the first two or three," gloated Trevor.

"Indeed. All good runs come to an end at some point and perhaps Amanda's unbeaten record is going to fall to you?" mused Rufus.

"Here's hoping," said Trevor "So let me tell you all about it."

After Trevor had recounted every painstaking detail Rufus meandered to the office that he shared with nobody else. However, he did deliberately stop by a colleague's room to place his wager of a bottle of Fonseca Vintage Port on Trevor to win by 'technical knockout'. He was pleased he used the correct phrase, but the other senior member of Chambers didn't appreciate the reference although he did accept the bet.

***

As pre-arranged Amanda called her Aunt and Uncle for their weekly catch up and natter. Her Aunt, as usual, spoke about the goings on in all the soap operas on television and normally Amanda would indulge the conversation by googling the story lines before they spoke. Her Uncle had no interest, but she knew that her Aunt did and it always meant there was a conversation to fall back on. This time they talked about a male character in one of the soaps that was struggling with his sexuality and how he didn't want to be snubbed by his mechanic best friend who, apparently, he was secretly in love with. Amanda's Aunt did most of the talking as usual and despite the potential for aged prejudice from her she was saying that she didn't understand why television had to make such a drama about being gay in the twenty first century. Amanda had tuned out really and just offered an understanding "mmm". Eventually she got on to more important matters by asking her Aunt how to get an orange juice stain out of a rug? Her Aunt, of course, knew the answer but before she could impart it "Hard work and effort" shouted her Uncle over the top of his wife as he tended to do, rather than actually speaking directly into the phone.

"Very good," replied Amanda, "but seriously how do I ..."

"Your Uncle is quite right my lovely." Amanda didn't take offence at lovely this time. "A tiny drop of washing up liquid, warm water, effort and lots of patience."

"Right," was the only response from Amanda but it was said with elongating the first syllable, so it sounded like "rrrright."

"Where is the stain, not on your Hadschlu rug?"

"Yep," confirmed Amanda

"Oh dear. I tell you what I'll pop over and sort it all out for you," offered her Aunt.

"Thank you. So how was the Opera?" Amanda asked. "Bloody terrible," cried out her Uncle.

The conversation jumbled along for a few more minutes and then Amanda remembered to ask her Uncle about who Churchill was referring to in his quote about a china shop and a bull. "John Foster Dulles" was the immediate answer "He was the US Secretary of State under President Eisenhower who …"

Both Amanda and her Aunt cut off the male voice before he could start an impromptu and unwanted lecture by chorusing "Nooo." Everyone chuckled at his playful bonhomie.

***

R v O'Ryan was listed before Judge Emily Brannigan at Nailton Crown Court for two days. The R denoted that The Crown was bringing the case against Ricky O'Ryan and when the first day fell on a Wednesday the Defendant was nervous and it showed.

Amanda did her level best to explain that he would be fine, and he was just to be honest. Her advice was as it should be but it was Phil's guidance that didn't help assuage any nerves "Agreed but don't speak too much either for fuck's sake – just answer the questions as briefly as you can". She consoled herself that Phil was doing his best too, as she drained the last of the froth from her recyclable cup that had contained her full fat milk, double shot and extra chocolate sprinkles large cappuccino coffee which she always had at the start of every trial. It had begun as a comfort blanket type of drink but having never lost a case she did not want to jinx anything, so it had quickly developed into a habit and one that she dared not break. Her other pre-trial ritual was a boxing workout with her personal trainer Zach, but early Wednesday's were his back-to-back classes, so she had to make do with a Tuesday morning session this time instead. Amanda worked hard and threw some healthily aggressive combinations as she imagined the punch bag to be Trevor's face.

It was late morning as the normal 10:30 start time had slipped back.

Judge Emily Brannigan shuffled into her seat and when she was ready, she indicated with a formal nod of her head to the court clerk that the trial could commence. As is the accepted process at Crown Court trials the Defendant states their intended plea. Ricky spoke in a clear and confident voice "Not Guilty." It was fortunate that he was again back in the dock for when he addressed the courtroom, he could feel his legs shake but they were hidden behind the wooden screen that rose around four foot from the floor.

The Jury was selected, as always, by random ballot from a collection who had funnelled into the court room having received a formal letter stating that they had been selected for duty. Most of them looked more than a little fed up as they approached the end of their two-week stint of jury service.

Unlike in the United States of America there was no

selection process and neither the prosecution nor the defence teams had any vetoes. It was literally the luck of the draw, but the supposed luck of the Irish had evidently deserted Ricky as eight women and only four men were chosen by the clerk to the court, Amanda had hoped for a male dominated jury or at least an equal split. The remainder of those still waiting to be allocated to a case returned to the holding area for more bitter tepid coffee and out-of-date magazines.

As the chosen twelve members of the jury stumbled along the rows of seats, like they were trying to leave a theatre halfway through a performance, Amanda tried to make eye contact. Other than one of the men, an elderly gent type who had dressed up for the occasion and was clearly going to take matters very seriously as he had an A4 pad of paper clutched under one elbow, everyone was focused on not tripping over in the narrow aisles. Amanda's attempt at non-verbal connection had not gone very well.

Trevor Hamper-Houghton was not a skilled advocate. He lacked the ability to adjust to the highs and lows of a trial. As he was prosecuting the case on behalf of the Crown Prosecution Service it was his turn first to present the case against the Defendant and his opening remarks set the tone he was aiming for.

"The threshold test to satisfy the Crown that Grievous Bodily harm with intent to cause GBH has been met." He solemnly bowed his head as if he had just announced the death of relative.

"The Defendant," he raised his index finger on his left hand and directed attention upon Ricky "is a professional boxer. He is paid to punch and inflict damage with his fists and on the day in question he punched the victim, who we will hear from in due course, so hard that he required extensive medical and dental treatment to repair the damage inflicted upon him by the Defendant."

Amanda rose, "allegedly," she challenged.

Judge Brannigan accepted the distinction as did Trevor who scribbled that word onto his speech that he was reading verbatim. He repeated his opening by adding in 'allegedly'.

The only comment that flashed across Stephen's mind, who was again seated in the public gallery but this time mindful of the desire to avoid another terrifying stare from the judge was 'Ricky is barely paid'. Stephen was sat next to a muscly good looking young man whose arms were covered in tattoos and so in order not to commit another faux-pax he spent most of the hearing staring at the inked images trying to work out what they all meant.

Amanda was all too aware of the requirements to prove the intent element of the charge. It was an obvious argument that Trevor was going to raise, and do so early, that an aggravating factor to try to satisfy the charge before the court, was the use of a weapon and given Ricky's profession the prosecution were going to try and persuade the jury that his fists were a potentially deadly weapon.

Trevor's opener was more of a beginning, middle and an end as it dragged on and on. His tone and pitch were all wrong, in Amanda's opinion, as he stood all but statue still and read from a pre-prepared and overly rehearsed speech. The only movements he made for the best part of an hour and a half, as he took everyone in earshot through every event of that night, was the occasional glance to the Judge and the turning over of page after page.

Amanda noted that some of the jury had drifted off to a vacant and distant land but the elderly gent who she mentally dubbed 'Mr Write' was writing as furiously as his arm would let him and not once did he look up or stop for a rest during the entirety of Trevor's monologue. She smiled warmly at Stephen who gave a very unsubtle thumbs up gesture back and her eyes were then drawn to the man sat next to him. They looked at each for little more than a second then he turned his gaze away.

Without even a pause in his inflection Trevor announced that he intended to call the Crown's witness. It came as a surprise to most as there was no discernible change in his voice or any obvious conclusion to his opening statement.

However, Judge Brannigan stopped him in his tracks as she declared that after a shortened morning and such a detailed opening that it was now the time to break for the lunch recess. This was greeted with approving rumbles from the stomachs of the jury.

There was little to analyse over the break from Amanda's point of view, but she poured over her notes as Phil and Stephen tried to guess how well the morning had gone.

Everyone took their places again feeling a little more energised after a well-earned break and some much-needed sustenance. Judge Brannigan surveyed the room and indicated to the prosecution legal team that the trial could resume.

At this moment a well-presented man slipped into the back corner of the public gallery. He was casually dressed in designer clothes but as he sat down, he pulled on a baseball cap and dark glasses and tried to hunker down in his seat to avoid detection. Judge

Emily Brannigan missed nothing.

"Counsel, before you proceed may I address the gentleman who has just entered the gallery."

Every single pair of eyes were now trained on the new arrival.

"There is to be no non-secular headwear in my court so if you wish to remain please remove it and the same goes for those glasses unless you can evidence a medical need for them to remain on."

The man was annoyed as he wanted to try to remain incognito but in trying too hard, he had actually brought more attention on himself.

Taking off the hat and the glasses the majority of the room did not recognise who was uncovered and this included both barristers and the judge.

Ricky, Stephen and Phil knew who it was straightaway.

Ethan Harris was a little redder in the face than usual after his public admonishment but there he was, not on the television screen this time but in the flesh.

Judge Brannigan returned to Trevor and indicated for him to continue. Stephen gave a double thumbs up and a toothy smile to Ethan who nodded back. Ricky was delighted that his promoter had come although it made him a little more nervous, but he made sure he mouthed 'thank you' when his and Ethan's eyes locked over the court room.

The victim of the alleged incident was smartly dressed in a classic slim fit dark navy suit. He confirmed his name as "Tom Southall". Tom was then sworn in and as he repeated the oath he spoke in a calm and confident voice. Amanda hoped that Ricky was paying attention to how a witness should conduct himself.

In careful response to the intricate questioning from Trevor his version of events, that ultimately led to him lying down on the cold concrete slabs outside The Circle House pub, were put before the court record. All twelve jurors especially Mr Write, paid particular attention to this evidence as it was the first time that they had heard what took place that Saturday night.

It all sounded very typical. Tom and a few friends had met earlier on a Saturday afternoon for a lazy lunch in London's West End. A couple of drinks over food and a few of that group had decided to make a night of it and stay out.

Amanda was crafting a question in her mind about how much alcohol Tom had consumed but Trevor cut off that line of re-interrogation with a simple question of his own to which Tom coolly responded "No, I was not drinking as I had to be on a train by eight am on Sunday to get to my nieces' christening."

"Diu," thought Amanda.

"Did you manage to attend the christening?" It was the obvious follow up from Trevor and Amanda knew the answer before it was given.

"Sadly, no. I was still in hospital, so I missed my train and the christening as well." It was a practiced response, but it was well delivered. Mr Write didn't miss getting it down on paper.

Trevor ticked his script with an over flamboyant swipe of his right hand.

"So, if I can take you back to that night?" lead Trevor. "You had not been drinking - that is correct?"

Amanda needed to try and break the rhythm because if the prosecution intended to conduct their case in such a painstaking way, they'd be under pressure to get their Defence in on time. Also as the trial was listed for only two days if it didn't finish on time the risk was twofold of securing a 'not guilty' verdict. The first being that the jury, as they were coming to the end of their two weeks service, would rush their deliberation and that tended to mean a 'guilty' outcome and the second was that at the speed Trevor was going the two days would fast evaporate and a split trial could occur where the defence and conclusion elements would have to wait until the court could find more availability and that posed the danger of a mis-trial as an entirely new jury may be required.

"Have we not already heard the witness' stated position in this regard?" interjected Amanda as she stood to her feet.

Judge Brannigan after a second or two of consideration responded, "Thank you Miss Buckingham but this is my court." Amanda dutifully nodded and sat back down.

"Mr Hamper-Houghton please proceed," and the Judge added "but I think it will be to everyone's benefit if we do not have to endure overly repetitive clarification questioning." "Yes of course" was all he could say.

Amanda's tactic worked.

The danger of total reliance on scripted advocacy is that when an event occurs that disrupts your flow or worse still when you are told that some of the planned future questions are not going to be accepted by the Judge it throws your entire momentum out.

This is what happened to Trevor.

Amanda took no satisfaction in watching her colleague struggle and fumble as he tried to regain his composure. His right hand was frantically, and far less ostentatiously than earlier, striking through question after question from his extensive list.

"So … er … and to move on …" Trevor was searching for something substantive to say next. Advocacy is a skill and you cannot effectively learn it from a book either.

Trevor cleared his throat and launched "So please tell the Court what you and your friends were thinking at the time?"

"Apologies to my learned friend but I cannot fathom how the witness will be able to correctly state under oath what his friends were thinking, surely he can only comment on what he was thinking." Amanda was not going to make it easy for Trevor.

"Yes of course, I am grateful for the assistance from my learned friend. What were you thinking at the time?" asked Trevor.

"At what time?" came the response from the witness stand.

Amanda looked down to her shiny shoes and couldn't stop a tiny curl of her lips. As she looked back up she glanced at the jury and annoyingly Mr Write had taken his first break from writing everything down and was watching the interaction between them as if he were sat at home in front of the television.

"Thank you, I meant what were you thinking at the time of the events."

Tom Southall was a nice guy, he had studied hard at school and university and had been working for a branch of 'BankInc', an American financial institution for a number of years. He had intended to ask his long-term girlfriend to marry him, but he had only yesterday evening found out that she had not been faithful to him when she went on a girls trip abroad last month. He might have forgiven one drunken indiscretion but apparently it was a lot more than one and with multiple men too.

Tom was waiting for his chance to tell his version of what happened that night and he was beginning to squirm a little as time passed-by and he had not really had his chance to speak yet.

"Do you mean how did I end up on the pavement outside the pub?" he replied back.

Amanda could not help but enjoy the way the tables seemed to have turned in that the witness was asking the barrister the questions.

Trevor was visibly uncomfortable. His blotchy face was reddening by the minute and there were speckles of light on his forehead and by both his eyes as the court room lights picked up drops of sweat.

"Please tell the court in your own words your version of what happened?" It was a poorly phrased question and Amanda wrote down 'your version' on her notepad. She noticed that Mr Write was yet to pick his pen back up.

Tom was relieved to get his moment, as soon as this was all over, he could get back to his flat in Balham, South London and purge every memory of his former love from his home. He would probably skip his bed and burn his mattress too, but that might mean a visit from the police for starting a fire and he'd had enough of the authorities for a while. He'd just pay someone to take it all away instead.

"My friends and I were in The Circle House pub just enjoying a normal Saturday night. There were five of us, myself and two boys and two women, we all work together in the same risk analysis department at work, when some blokes came over and tried to chat up the girls," began Tom. Amanda noted the makeup of the group and thought, whilst Tom spoke eruditely, his choice of boys and women probably underlined the fact that he was still a boy himself and not yet a man.

"It was all harmless to begin with," continued Tom. "BankInc, where I work, aren't that keen on relationships between colleagues and I had a girlfriend at the time so the girls I was with were happy to play along."

Amanda noted down "at the time."

Mr Write was back hard at it too.

"It seemed that everything was fine but when we were being asked to leave the pub the girls headed downstairs to the toilet and then it just seemed to get out of hand really quickly."

"Please continue," said Trevor and then he added "take your time."

"Well we all got up to leave but waited at the top of the stairs off the main bar for the girls to come back but there was not enough room for us all. It was quite rowdy and my two friends and the other two got a little heated and someone fell against the exit door and it swung open. They all fell out into the street and I went out into the doorway to try to stop it closing but it was one of those heavy security doors with the push bar release thingies." As he described the internal release mechanisms, he pushed his hands down to indicate what he meant.

"Go on," encouraged Trevor.

"Then there was a scuffle to try and get back inside and get to the girls." Tom took a deep breath. "I managed to hold the door open for me to get back inside just as the girls came up the stairs and they then came out the door right past me."

The court room was silent as they waited to hear

what Tom said next. Stephen was holding his hands in the standard prayer position. Amanda's pen was at the ready as was Mr Write's. Ethan Harris leant forward in anticipation and even Judge Brannigan craned her head nearer to the witness stand to make sure she didn't miss what came next.

It was a let-down and more than a little disappointing.

"The door shut against my back and he told me to leave, well sort of," said Tom.

"Sort of?" questioned Trevor.

"He swore at me," Tom clarified.

"What did he say exactly?" Trevor asked

Tom was reluctant to use the words, so Trevor reassured him "It's okay to use profanities if you are repeating what you heard."

Tom nodded and with some satisfaction he said in open court "He told me to fuck off." There were a few sniggers around the room, but Judge Brannigan's Gatling Gun rapidity of icy stares soon restored quiet.

"And who was this he?" queried Trevor.

Tom looked directly at Ricky in the witness box and confirmed in a single word "him."

"For the benefit of the court please let it be noted that the witness has identified the accused."

Amanda sprung to her feet and pleading said, "But only identified him as swearing!" Exasperated Amanda hoped that Mr Write and the other eleven jury members had understood her point. Judge Brannigan seemed to but only offered "Thank you Miss Buckingham."

"Please continue with what happened next," prodded Trevor.

"So, then I was bumped a bit forward as the door

was trying to close behind me and I looked back over my shoulder for a split second then I felt my face explode in pain and then the next thing I knew I was flat on my back outside."

"Thank you, stepped in Trevor "I appreciate that having to relive this awful ordeal must have been very difficult indeed." Amanda rolled her eyes.

"Please may I turn everyone's attention to the video screen?" The barrister pointed to the large display on the opposite wall to where the jury sat. The only person who really had to stretch to see the screen was Ethan Harris who was still sat in the farthest corner.

Trevor had chosen to play the entire reel showing the melee outside and then the exiting girls followed by the all but flying Tom. The clip then paused, and Trevor went for the knockout blow.

"Immediately after the witness being assaulted and knocked to the floor, out stepped ..." he stopped speaking and pressed play.

Ricky walked out and towards his friends. He looked back into the pub as the door closed and then down at the prostrate Tom.

Murmurs and chunters echoed around, and they seemed to all be saying "well that's that then."

Trevor then read out the injuries suffered to Tom which included a fractured jaw, two lost teeth and a bloody nose. Tom showed the court room the gaps in his mouth. He had actually had a little bit of result because he worked for an American firm and as he was clearly the victim here they had very generously agreed, under his private health and dental care cover, to provide for him, free of charge, whatever treatment was needed. So he was going to get a brand-new smile out of this and given the heart-break he had suffered at the hands of his girlfriend, a new smile was definitely something to smile about.

More mutterings were heard.

Trevor then added one question too many. "So, in your opinion who inflicted these injures on you?"

Tom said one final word "him," and he pointed to Ricky once more.

With a satisfied nod of his head towards the witness stand Trevor sat down in his seat and reached for a glass of water.

Amanda serenely rose to her feet and smiled warmly at Tom, but she made sure that she didn't show off to him her beautiful set of pearly white teeth.

"Would you like a glass of water?" was her opening question. It was such a disarming one and Tom having said yes was provided with a plastic beaker full of a liquid that resembled H_2O. It was most certainly not bottled mineral water sourced from the picturesque mountain ranges of Scotland but from a toilet tap next to the Judge's robing room.

"I am conscious of your time Mr Southall so I will keep this very brief," spoke Amanda.

"You said your version of events earlier, so you therefore accept that there exist other versions too?"

Tom was puzzled.

"Erm," was all he could say.

"You accept that your version is your version and that therefore others will have their versions too, which may not be the same as yours don't you?"

"Yes," came the hesitant response.

"Thank you," confirmed Amanda. "So having agreed that your version is only one possible interpretation of these events do you also accept that having turned away before you were struck means you didn't actually see the Defendant commit what he is accused off?"

"…" Silence was all Tom could offer.

"May I remind the Court that the Defendant has pleaded Not Guilty," added Amanda.

"He was there," offered Tom.

"Indeed, but there is a vast difference between being there and being guilty of the charge levied against the Defendant."

Amanda sat down and received a series of slightly over energetic pats on the back from Phil.

"With that, as it is almost that time of the day I suggest that we reconvene at half past ten tomorrow morning," declared Judge Brannigan who then reminded Ricky that he was still under caution and that the jury were not permitted to discuss this matter with anyone and that included family members.

Ethan was first back through security and outside in the hope of not having to wait for a taxi, but he fell straight into a series of flashbulbs as cameras went off and then the interrogations from reporters followed like gunfire. Questions to the left of him, questions to the right of him and a wall of pushing and shoving cameramen in front.

"Why are you here Mr Harris?"

"Can I have quote please Ethan?"

It was almost impossible for the normally calm promoter to hear the barrage of things asked of him let alone respond to anyone of them. There was one question though that made him stop dead in his tracks.

"Do you not think that Mr O'Ryan should have in actual fact been charged twice for GBH with intent given the assault occasioned to Kris Baker during your boxing show?"

Ethan replied "There is a fundamental difference between licenced professional sport and these events, but let us be crystal clear, Ricky said he is not guilty and until something changes he is not guilty and I firmly believe that to be the case." He attracted the attention of a waiting taxi who turned on his lights and engine and began to creep forward towards Ethan's direction. "As for any disparaging of the noble art of boxing I think that is entirely unreasonable and suggests a deep and ingrained misunderstanding of the sport."

With that he opened the cab door and dived in, as if he were in an action movie declaring to the driver "Get me outta here!"

Ethan looked back over his shoulder and was glad to get away from that media scrum. He was also suitably impressed with how he handled those unexpected questions. Ethan then made a couple of calls and tempting fate one of them one was to Northern Ireland.

Amanda brushed off the plaudits and wanted to get back home to prepare for the next day when Ricky would take the stand. Phil took Ricky and Stephen back to their hotel, which was practically their permanent residence given the nights spent there. Ricky hoped that there was not going to be another small room for him as his permanent residence tomorrow.

***

Amanda opened the door to her flat and walked in. The smell of fresh flowers still greeted her, and it made her smile as did the spotless Louis De Poortere Hadschlu rug. Her Aunt was such a kind person and cleaning the carpet must have taken her hours and Amanda could not even tell where the stain had been. Leaving flowers was a lovely touch too. Amanda told herself not to forget their regular Wednesday night chat.

Still smiling she called out for Rumpole who waddled into the living room and meowed for food. The cat and his mistress ate together. One had salmon the other had chicken but neither really enjoyed their meal.

Several hours of hard prep work later Amanda was sat at her ornate desk and leaning back for a well-earned stretch she decided on a quick break and a call with her Aunt and Uncle.

She snuggled down on her sofa next to Rumpole who was a little grumpy that he no longer had exclusive possession. Amanda dialled the telephone number and to her surprise and delight her Uncle answered the phone and he didn't pass it immediately over. "How are you darling?" he enquired.

"Good, I'm good thank you. How are you?" It was a perfunctory conversation but no different from the start of every family telephone call up and down the country. Before they could move on from the opening pleasantries there was a squeal of delight from her Aunt that Amanda could easily hear down the line "Put her on, put her on," her Aunt called out. "I think your Aunt has something important that she wants to talk to you about."

Amanda could hear the phone being passed over and then her Aunt began to talk at a thousand miles an hour about the latest goings-on in that soap opera and how the expression of love from the man to his mechanic best friend had not gone well. Her Aunt then described almost word for word how the drama had unfolded and a line that she said had been perfectly written "I can't be the version of myself that you want me to be, I've got to be my own version of myself and my version loves you and I want to be with you."

"What did you just say?" butted in Amanda. Her Aunt repeated herself "I love you and I want to be with you."

"No no no, before that."

"Err … now let me think … Ah yes … er … " the wait was excruciating "I can't be the version of myself that you want me to be, I've got to be my own version of myself and …"

Amanda almost fell of the sofa as she jumped up. Rumpole tumbled over into the dent in the cushion left by his owner.

"There is more than one version!" shouted Amanda "Look I am sorry, but I have to go."

"Okay," said her Aunt but Amanda didn't even hear that as she was already heading to her desk and her notes of that day's trial. The phone line had disconnected, and Amanda went to her Uber App and placed a booking for an immediate cab. She rushed to her dressing room and having tied up her blondish hair in to a bun she pulled on a baseball hat that she had picked up from an American Football game she had been dragged to by her Uncle at Wembley Stadium a few months back. Next Amanda pulled on some tight fitting jeans, a jumper and an over-sized hooded top; the latter was normally reserved for those cold winter days when she wanted to sit hunched with her knees to her chin and pull the garment down to her ankles. She then went to the top of her eight-drawer cabinet and at the back there was a solitary orange trainer-sock which had inside it a few hundred pounds in cash. She stuffed a few notes into her left jeans pocket and to do so she pulled out her mobile phone which pinged at her at that very moment to tell her that her cab had arrived.

The journey from Clerkenwell to the West End is a pleasant journey but Amanda didn't pay any attention. There was no conversation at all other than when she had confirmed her destination.

The Circle House pub was busy for a Wednesday late evening and Amanda, having apologised for not having any loose change to the driver, walked inside. It was the first time she had been there and looking around she had a rather strange sensation of having had the layout described to her in court earlier that day and it made her feel like she had walked into a re-creation of the pub rather than the real one.

At the bar she recognised the person serving the drinks and waiting for him to serve her specifically took a little while but eventually Amanda heard him say to her "What can I get you?"

"The truth," Amanda ordered

"Vermouth?" was the surprised response.

Amanda leant forward as far over the bar as she could without actually sitting on top of it and whispered, "The truth," into the barman's ear. He stepped back and looked carefully into Amanda's face and saw the same eyes he had seen earlier that day.

"Hey Sam?" he called down the bar to his colleague "sorry mate I need five." With that he opened the hatch and walked around to Amanda. "Not here," he pulled her arm and led her off towards the staircase to the toilets.

As had been described, but missed by most at the trial that day, there was an internal door that led up to the accommodation above the pub. The eight-digit security code was punched in and the door opened outward as Amanda suspected it would and the two walked up a steep set of uneven stairs to the digs above the pub.

The main communal room fanned out across the large bay window that Amanda had previously noticed when she first walked past on her way to Charing Cross Police Station, which seemed like a lifetime ago.

The barman offered Amanda a drink, but she declined.

They stood in the room with both of them not really knowing what to say.

Amanda took control. "So, something got me thinking earlier. You sat through court today but why were you there?"

The man crossed his muscly tattooed arms in an attempted show of defiance.

"I can tell you why if you'd prefer?" declared Amanda confidently.

***

Nailton Court the following day was buzzing. The press and paparazzi loitered around the entrance. Amanda and Phil were looked at with interest and a few snap-happy reporters took a photo or two. When Ricky and Stephen emerged from the same taxi interest in Amanda and Phil increased but the majority of the media attention was directed on Ricky. Stephen did his best to shield the boxer and get him inside without delay "Confident of going home today Ricky?" was one of the questions that was screamed as they passed. Ricky didn't reply but he thought 'I fucking hope so'.

Ethan Harris was late. Day Two was under way by the time he arrived. Rather than trying to go under the radar like yesterday, which had spectacularly failed, he had his chauffeur driven car take him but only after they had detoured via London City Airport to meet a flight in from Belfast.

Mrs O'Ryan was sat next to her eldest daughter Skye in the back of Ethan Harris's chauffer driven Bentley. They had talked about nothing else but Ricky and the case for the entire journey to court. Being late the press numbers had dwindled a little as they had dispersed in the hunt for a greasy spoon café but a few remained with their flasks and sausage rolls in hand so the gauntlet into court was far less arduous than Ethan had feared.

After heading through security, which was a unique experience for both Mrs O'Ryan and Skye, Ethan led them to the court doors and smiled at them both as he opened the door and ushered them towards the public gallery. Stephen gave another thumbs up to Ethan but he was shocked to see Ricky's mother and sister.

Ricky was stood in the witness stand and he felt as if he wanted the ground to open up and swallow him whole as he saw two of the three late arrivals.

Amanda had been gently offering reassuring questions to him like "Boxing is a sport of great restraint is it not?" and "You are aware of the consequences for your career of inappropriate actions." Trevor tried to inject and suggest that this line of questioning was not relevant but Amanda explained to him, Judge Brannigan, Mr Write and the other eleven jurors that character was actually an important factor in assessing the mind of the Defendant. A better advocate would have robustly challenged this statement but Trevor, despite being urged to by Lorna Williams from behind his seat, failed to do so.

Ricky was waiting for the question and eventually it came "Did you punch the victim?"

"No, I did not," came the confident reply that everyone was expecting.

No one was expecting her next question "How can you be so certain that you didn't?" As hard as Lorna Williams had tried to encourage Trevor a few moments earlier Phil was now desperately trying to stop Amanda.

Amanda had the arrogance to stand there looking straight at Ricky and the confidence to style it out. In private Amanda would joke, when she was asked 'how do you stand up in front of so many people and not go to pieces?', that she either had the arrogance to fake the confidence or the confidence to fake the arrogance.

Here at Nailton Crown Court with the entire attention focused on her, and why she had asked that question and why had she spent the first half an hour of her opening talking about character, Amanda stood as the perfect image of a brilliant and confident barrister.

Ricky was struggling with how to respond, "Because I didn't," was all he could offer.

Amanda then chose to do something that she had never thought she would ever do, and it was against everything she learnt at University and Law School.

She cross-examined her own witness.

Trevor couldn't believe his luck. After a disappointing end to Day One his opponent was clearly committing case and career suicide.

Lorna managed to get hold of his shoulder and pull him back towards her. She hissed into his ear "She knows something." Trevor turned his head just enough to whisper back but so that his eyes were still on

Amanda "No, she's trying to get him some sympathy from the jury. It's an old trick but not a good one."

Amanda was tough with her clients when she had to be, but she would prefer a more collaborative approach, but this was not one of those times.

"Why can you be so certain?"

"Because I am," Ricky snapped back.

Amanda kept going.

"Not good enough for me or this court and you know it."

Trevor rose "I am not sure my learned friend should be addressing the witness in such a manner." Before Judge Brannigan could comment Amanda turned on Trevor "It is my witness."

There was nothing left for the judge to do other than to shrug her shoulders in acquiescence of Amanda's conduct for she was quite correct. Brannigan was curious as to what was going to happen next, so she motioned for these extraordinary events to continue.

"One last time I ask you how you can be so certain that you did not throw the punch?" pressed Amanda.

"I just am," snapped back Ricky.

"That hair trigger temper of yours will get you into some trouble one of these days," came back Amanda.

Stephen shook his head in disbelief, Ethan Harris stared at Phil who just threw his hands up in desperation as if he were declaring to the watching world "What is this person doing, she is meant to be on our side!" Even Mr Write had stopped taking notes as he and the rest of the jury watched the Defence barrister attack the Defendant.

"I have the impression Ricky that you are holding back a piece of information that if divulged would in all probability clear you of the crime you have been accused of committing." Amanda paused before she added "I know what that is, and I ask you whether you want me to tell everyone or whether you want to say it yourself?"

"You haven't got a clue," retorted Ricky.

"I have and I have proof too."

Trevor jumped up "New evidence! I had to listen to groundless allegations regarding my evidence and yet the Defence may …"

"You mean the Crown's evidence, don't you?" interrupted Amanda.

"Yes, yes of course I do," said Trevor angrily.

"You have no reason to be concerned as this evidence is not directly related to this case."

Trevor looked even more confused than usual.

Amanda, just as if it were as easy as turning off a tap, altered her tone. "Ricky, I am on your side here." Everyone including Ricky looked surprised at this statement given the last few minutes of total grilling that he had just endured.

"The reality of this case is simple. You are at real risk of forfeiting a very promising career because you are too scared to allow the true version of yourself to come out and you'd rather be a version that others want you to be."

Amanda placed her left hand into her trouser pocket and from it was produced a yellow lanyard and she placed it over her neck. The metallic clip that would normally hold an identification card was empty. She turned and draped it over the side of her desk as if it were a random object that she had unexpectedly found and was now discarding it. The few that noticed concluded it that way.

Ricky didn't though as he recognised his lanyard.

Amanda looked at Ricky. She then turned her gaze upon the barman who was sat near Stephen in the gallery. She stared back at Ricky as his head slumped and added "I have the I.D. too."

"I can't," he whimpered.

"I'm sorry I didn't quite catch that?" said Judge Brannigan.

Amanda spoke to Ricky as if it were just the two of them in the room. "Ricky is it really something to throw your career away for?"

Nobody said anything for what seemed an eternity.

Ricky's face was wet with the tears that were now streaming down his face. His mum stood and wanted to console her son. Skye, his sister, did her best to ease their mother's anxiety. They were both crying too.

Stephen had no idea what was going on. Phil had long ago decided to sit back and watch events unfold before him like a live soap opera. The members of the jury were transfixed and as for Trevor he had an impending feeling he was about to lose his first prosecution case for the CPS.

Amanda said one final thing before Ricky burst into voice. "I can promise you Ricky whatever you think is the worst thing that will happen by keeping your silence is incomparable to what could happen to you in prison and will happen to your boxing career."

He slowly nodded and then more assertedly as he finally returned Amanda's gaze.

For the final time she asked, "Why are you so certain you are not guilty?"

"I didn't throw the punch because someone else did." Trevor was exasperated "Is that it?" he cried out from his seat.

"Ignore him Ricky, talk to me," Amanda beseeched.

"I had been upstairs and only came down when I heard noises that sounded like a fight was going to kick off."

"Upstairs in the pub?" clarified Amanda.

"Yes," came the reply.

"Were you alone?" Amanda delicately phrased the question knowing that she probably had one chance to get this absolutely right.

"No," was the monosyllabic response.

"Who were you with?" Amanda needed to try to get more than just one word answers out of Ricky.

There was silence.

Ricky looked at his mother and she smiled back at him and then blew him a kiss.

Ricky lowered his head ever so slightly and announced to the expectant audience "I was upstairs with one of the bar staff."

No one moved an inch as their brains were trying to work out what the significance of this rather peculiar exchange was going to have on proceedings.

"Could you be more specific?" Amanda spoke with compassion and also a twinge of desperation.

"I was with him," blurted out Ricky as he pointed to the tattooed man in the gallery.

Heads shot left and right and right and left from Ricky to the barman, who had sunk as deep into his chair as he could, but the only two that remained still and focused on Ricky were Amanda's and his mother's. The latter smiled and mouthed to him a few maternal words "I knew, I always knew so don't fret my Star Man."

Judge Brannigan was howling for quiet from the bench which just added to the general sense of disorder in her courtroom. Eventually the noise subsided, and Amanda was able to ask her final question "Tell us what really happened Ricky?"

***

The trial of R v O'Ryan ended in no less dramatic fashion than Amanda's interrogation of her own witness.

The Crown's evidence ultimately fell apart. Ricky and the barman were together upstairs when the commotion was heard below. The boxer was first down the stairs and when Tom had tried to re-enter the pub through the side door it was Ricky who had told him to "fuck off." The barman, who threw the punch, just as Tom averted his gaze, had come flying down the stairs, late onto the scene for he had literally been caught with his trousers down and just launched a fist forward into the side of Tom's face.

The barman was technically guilty of an offence, but the CPS declined to proceed against him even though Trevor offered his services for free. The barman continued to work in the Circle House pub, but he never saw Ricky again and nor did Trevor hear anything from Lorna or the CPS either.

Connor and Michael drifted into obscurity in their relationship with Ricky. It had nothing to do with Ricky being openly gay but more to do with the fact that he realised the only thing that Connor and Michael brought to their relationship was grief.

Rufus tried to argue that gambling debts are generally unenforceable but along with the bet he lost that argument too. The bottle of Vintage Fonseca Port was by no means the most expensive on offer, but it

143

wasn't cheap either. He had hoped that the winner would at least offer him a tipple but that didn't happen. Rufus would have been furious if he had ever found out that the bottle ultimately ended up on a wine tombola at a village fete.

Dave and Amanda's professional relationship went from strength to strength after yet another win for the star at Hartington Chambers. Phil continued to send in work whenever he could, and he only ever wanted Amanda; they even went for several drinks on many occasions and he learnt how to smile properly.

As for Trevor, he and Amanda felt it was the right time to spread their respective wings and after Dave had undergone a series of intense negotiations he was able to move them both to new rooms in order that one didn't feel mistreated in having to leave whilst the other stayed. They remained professionally courteous to each other, but they never met for lunch again and Trevor never advocated at a trial on his own ever again.

Amanda received the plaudits as well as a private telling off from Dave for heading to the Circle House pub unaccompanied for if the barman was so ready to lash out once he might have done it again. As always Amanda deflected the praise back on the real star of the court room. Ricky, she described as The Star Witness, and he rightly left court a free man; in more senses than just one. Dave asked Amanda a few days later how she knew how to win? She just replied simply that when she was upstairs Ricky's lanyard and I.D. tag was hanging off a pin board in the lounge as a further memento of the barman's extensive collection of conquests. It cost her £150 pounds and a promise for the barman to attend court the next day but in the end, it was money well spent.

Ricky's sexuality created a lot of media attention in Great Britain and in Northern Ireland. His deep-seated fears of being cast adrift by his family and his Catholic community never happened. As for his fellow professional boxers, with the exception of a tiny fistful of narrow-minded bigots, they didn't care. Ricky became a standard bearer for other LGBTQ+ sportspeople. Stephen continued to manage and train him and Ethan Harris promoted him all the way to a World Championship bout, which he won and so Ricky returned to Belfast a national hero with his own O'Ryan's belt.

THE END

BONUS CONTENT

Season 1: Case 1
The Courageous Witness

Sarah Tomkins said "No!" and had meant it. She pleaded with the prosecuting barrister, Amanda Buckingham, to believe her. Amanda feared that some of the jury had already made up their minds that Sarah had consented, and they would find the two accused men not guilty.

The trial had not gone well for Amanda, one of the rising stars of the Bar. She knew she was going to have to face her own demons for Sarah to get what she was so desperate for — justice.

THE COURAGEOUS WITNESS

It was a size too big for her. That was why she was wearing it.

Amanda wrapped the pink-flowered cheongsam around her naked body. In the privacy of her Clerkenwell flat, in the hour past midnight, she felt secure in the protective 'long shirt'. She was sipping hot water which, according to ancient Chinese medicine, stimulated blood flow around the body and had restorative healing qualities. She had a throbbing headache and was ready to try anything to shift it.

Amanda curled up on her sofa which was far too big for her flat. She was not comfortable but staying in the foetal position seemed to ease her stress. She was reading a policy document produced by the Crown Prosecution Service. After yawning, she stood up and stretched her aching limbs. She walked into her kitchen to check that Rumpole's water bowl was full. As she did so, she glanced at the digital clock on her oven. With a sigh, Amanda knew she had to go to bed if she was to function in the morning, but she was acutely aware that the last hour or so of reading had been mostly ineffectual – unless by some sheer miracle she had retained information through osmosis.

Filling Rumpole's water bowl and sprinkling a perfect dozen cat biscuits into his favourite bowl, Amanda focused her mind on the CPS document about the prosecution of rape cases:

Rape is one of the most serious of all criminal offences. It can inflict lasting trauma on victims and their families.

And:

The majority of rape victims are women and most know their rapist.

Sarah Tomkins certainly knew the two men charged with her assault. She knew them extremely well.

Rape also has a devastating effect on families of the victims.

Amanda returned to the sofa, lost in memories that sent a shiver through her. She shook her head to try to push them deep back inside. With a groan of discomfort as her headache refused to ease, she returned to the papers.

The CPS realises that victims of rape have difficult decisions to make that will affect their lives and the lives of those close to them.

Amanda had read all of the evidence several times previously and she was still unsure as to why Sarah was refusing anonymity and was focusing on her day in court. Amanda concluded that Sarah was after revenge – and public revenge at that.

The law does not require the victim to have resisted physically in order to prove lack of consent. The question of whether the victim consented is a matter for the jury to decide.

Amanda looked up from her laptop and stared straight ahead as she recited the provisions of The Sexual Offences Act 2003;

The defendant must show that his belief in consent was reasonable.

Amanda was thinking hard and had almost forgotten about her headache. She turned back to the CPS document and decided to reread what she felt certain was the most important passage of all:

Proving the absence of consent is usually the most difficult part of a rape prosecution and is the most common reason for a rape case to fail. Prosecutors will look for evidence such as injury, struggle or immediate distress to help them.

Amanda's immediate challenge was clear, unlike her head that was now beset with a thick fog because of the absolute refusal of her headache to ease. She was simply unable to shake her belief that it was going to be difficult – very difficult – to convince a jury that Sarah Tomkins was the victim of a sexual assault by two men and, in the case of one of them, rape. Amanda was racked by tormented memories that she could no longer repress. Despite her sub-conscious efforts, these were racing around her pulsating head like fireflies and she was struggling to concentrate.

You'll feel better after a good night's sleep was always the advice from her Aunt Eileen. There was no chance of a good night's sleep and Amanda knew it. Her brain was aching as it leapt from thought to thought but, with each passing moment, she started to lose the last remnants of focus as she began to muddle the facts of Sarah Tomkins' case with her own bitter memories.

Amanda fell onto her bed and underwent the fight with the duvet and the scatter cushions as she struggled to get comfortable. Eventually, after a considerable and over-elaborate effort, she was able to wiggle herself down and under the covers. Following two meaningful punches to her pillows, she finally closed her eyes.

A second or so after doing so, a thought came to her. Had she fed Rumpole? She couldn't remember but she knew that if she hadn't, he'd be walking all over her and purring into her ear in just a few minutes.

Amanda kicked the covers off. With a loud cry of

"*Diu!*" she stomped into the kitchen. In the half-light of the London night she could see her pet with his face in his food bowl, scoffing his late evening meal.

Amanda spun on her heels and went back to bed but was not quite as comfortable as before. She was giving in to exhaustion – but then the events that haunted her earlier began to replay in her mind.

He had come up behind her, totally unexpectedly. Despite her judo training from Fat FrEthan in Kowloon, she was helpless as he forced her over.

Rumpole came and joined Amanda on the bed, curling up between her knees and elbows. She, though half asleep, placed a hand over his stomach. She failed to realise from his breathing patterns that not all was well with her fat cat.

A few weeks earlier, Sarah Tomkins had been lying prostrate on her back on the boardroom table. She could feel the hard surface irritating the skin of her buttocks. Ethan was penetrating her as Ivan, watching from the side, was gathering his breath and pulling up his trousers.

"She likes it rough," he gasped. "Have your fill, Ethan."

Sarah was numb; her mind had switched off and she was unable to register anything. She lay powerless with Ethan – sweaty, odious and panting – on top of her. Around the boardroom were cheap, non-matching chairs that had been upturned around the room a few minutes earlier.

The table and chairs belonged to a vehicle distribution company. It dealt in sales and its management meetings focused on sales figures. It didn't matter that the room lacked warmth, and nothing matched or showed a co-ordinated brand identity. Craig Heaton, the company's founder and chairman, didn't care. He only cared about profit and he had a fierce reputation for sacking staff for not reaching their often almost impossible targets.

Ivan was a senior salesman at Heaton Van Sales. He had brought in a significant order – worth close to a half million pounds – for supplying a fleet of custom transit vans. His success had been announced in the very room he was now getting dressed in, and which resulted in an impromptu party that had started three hours earlier in the staff kitchen on the ground floor of Heaton House.

Ethan, Ivan's devoted subordinate, had supported him faithfully like a lapdog throughout the four months of endless negotiations up to the contract being signed. The order invoiced out at £488,887. Ivan's bonus was 5% of the total, so a smidgen under £24,500 of which he gave £4,000 to Ethan, £1,500 to Luca, an assistant salesman (who played a key role in securing the deal), £400 to Sarah and £200 each to her three colleagues on reception. Ivan still cleared almost £18,000 on one order and this was on top of his basic pay.

When Craig, who was at his beachside apartment in the Canary Islands, heard that the customer had paid in full, he walked round the swimming pool with a bottle of champagne, making sure that everyone knew he had landed another deal. It was, of course, down to him as usual, he boasted, but in reality, he didn't even know the names of some of his staff, let alone the precise details of the deals they were doing. It was always about the bottom line with him; about the money in the bank, nothing else. His reply to London was short but exultant:

'Brilliant performance. It's party time: no limits. C.'

Craig liked to sign off every internal email, message or memorandum with a capital C. However, it didn't stand for Craig but for chairman. It was important that everyone knew he was in charge even though he was rarely in the office. As he sat down on one of the empty loungers around his beachfront apartment, he cast a disinterested look over the beach. A semi-naked bathing beauty turned over on her sunbed and he found himself wondering if Sarah would hang around for the party he'd just authorised. He liked Sarah; he even recalled her name. Mind you, most men who met her didn't quickly forget her.

His thoughts about Sarah slowly disappeared. After all, he'd never make it back in time for the party. As he turned back away from the splendid sea view, his gold signet ring sparkled in the late afternoon sun. People always assumed that the jewel-encrusted C stood for Craig. It didn't, of course; it stood for chairman.

Back at Heaton Van Sales, alcohol and food had been delivered by the same high-end grocery business that had just agreed their order for a fleet of transit vans. Ivan told everyone who would listen that it was his order. Luca didn't mind; after all, no-one in the office would believe him over Ivan anyway, and it was better to be with Ivan than against him.

As is traditional at office parties, there was far more booze than food. It was not clear who brought in the 'powder'. The repair shop was the likely source although, with the appearance of a number of 'guests' including blonds, brunettes and redheads, their later protests of innocence were accepted. As it was, a few of the staff spent more time in the toilets than they did dancing in the foyer and on the kitchen tables. The women on reception sorted the music by setting up a playlist on a smart phone.

Their office celebrations were quite regular events, but Ivan was keen to make this, one to remember. He wanted everyone to know that he was a dynamic salesman and his parties were the best, especially as Craig was not there to steal his thunder.

There was booze, some food, music, drugs and girls: the party had begun.

Sarah was the head receptionist. She had helped to transform her team into an efficient, professional 'front-facing' part of the Heaton Van Sales machine. She always paid close attention to her appearance and she insisted that all 'her girls' did likewise. Her mantra was: "We are the first people customers see. We must greet them with courtesy and politeness, and always look professional". It would never be the catchphrase of the year, but she really did believe it.

It helped that she and 'her girls' regarded themselves as good-looking. In her case, that was not in question.

Sarah was enjoying the party; she always did. She stayed away from the coke – it wasn't her thing, and never had been, but she accepted that others partook. She had joined in the dancing with enthusiasm, eating little of what was on offer but drinking a lot of vodka and tonic. She was currently without a serious partner. She was happy to wait for one and to date casually in the interim.

Everyone knew that Sarah liked Ivan and Ivan liked Sarah. The flirtatious banter that passed between them over the receptionists' desk was devoid of subtlety most of the time and occasionally was downright lascivious. Neither seemed too fussed that Ivan was married with a child.

As the early evening celebrations began to unravel into the usual drunken shenanigans, Sarah, who had danced with Ivan a lot, at times very closely indeed, suggested to him that they have a more private party. She had surveyed her colleagues who were either wobbly, playing tonsil hockey or hurrying back and forth to the toilets, and had decided that it was time for a bit of fun. He was not exactly a 'newbie' to adultery and did not need any encouragement.

They slipped away from the mayhem and headed for the stairs that led to the boardroom. Ivan gestured for Ethan to come with him.

The fourth of their little group was the ever-present Luca. Apart from running around getting them drinks and taking away their empties, he'd never been more than six feet away from Ivan from the moment the music started. Ivan caught Luca's eye and mouthed "Piss off," to him, gesturing back towards the party.

Ivan and Sarah were giggling like teenagers as they stumbled and fumbled up the stairs. Ethan was half a dozen steps behind them, trying to catch a glimpse of forbidden flesh up Sarah's skirt. Against the wall by the boardroom door, Ivan and Sarah began to embrace. There was no element of sensitivity or subtlety; it was simply animalistic desire.

Ethan walked past them both and into the boardroom.

Sarah and Ivan stopped. Wiping her mouth with the back of her hand Sarah gasped,

"Get rid of him, Ivan, now!"

"We're a team, Sarah, me and Ethan. You've had

your bonus – now it's our turn."

He pushed her into the boardroom, grabbing her backside as he did so.

"That's a fine bit of ass you've got there," he crowed, kicking the door behind him.

As it banged shut, Ethan slurred,

"Remember the porn we watched the other night? Those two blokes and the nurse."

"It wasn't as good as that Japanese lot in the sauna," roared Ivan, high-fiving Ethan.

Sarah was sobering up – and was becoming concerned. She went for the door but, before she could escape, found herself being dragged back across the room and held down on the table. Ethan and Ivan pulled at her clothes. She cried out as her bra was ripped off.

"Please, no," she pleaded.

"I'll go first," growled Ivan as he pulled down her knickers.

Ethan held her as his colleague wiggled down his trousers. Sarah could not understand how Ivan, who she had really fancied, could be metamorphosing into the hefty, panting lump now forcing himself on top of her. She didn't try to resist. She couldn't, as every ounce of fight she thought she had vanished in the sheer terror of the moment. Ivan then had sex with her and slid off the table.

Sarah felt Ethan's grip on her arms relax. She opened her eyes. Ethan loomed up in front of her. Sarah feared that he was going to rape her. Desperately, she tried to climb away but he pushed her down on to the wooden surface. Her head crashed against the frame.

"No!" she screamed aloud.

When she tried to scream again, one of the men shoved his hand into her face. She struggled, but he was too strong for her. Sarah fought back and managed a split second of freedom which was just long enough for her to gasp for air. The next thing she felt was a fist hitting the side of her head. She winced in pain and momentarily lost consciousness. Then the hand returned to her mouth more brutally than before. The tears were uncontrollable as she felt herself being penetrated.

Summoning all her strength she made one final effort to escape but the two men just shoved her back down with the same care they'd treat an overfull wheelie bin.

Panicking, she opened her eyes and saw Ivan watching her, leering, his face sweaty and red.

"Fuck her good, Ethan," he screeched.

Sarah began to shake with revulsion.

Ethan withdrew. He then ran both his hands up her legs and pinched her inner thighs. Sarah's eyes bulged and she yelled out in pain. Ethan laughed and squeezed her flesh again.

Sarah turned her head to one side and tried to retch. Ivan grabbed Ethan and said, "Nice one, mate. You head back down; I'll be down in five."

Ivan moved back to Sarah and tried to re-arrange her blouse. Wild-eyed, Sarah fended him off with frantic hands. She slid off the table, so she was leaning against it, and pulled down her skirt. One of her bra straps had broken, but she managed to fasten the buttons on her blouse. Her shoes were a few feet in front of her.

Ivan suggested, "Let's get back to the party."

Sarah stopped dead in her tracks with one hand on

the back of a poorly veneered wooden chair. She stared at him in utter disbelief as her contempt began to show.

"You do what you want, but I'm calling the police," she said.

Ivan laughed.

"Will you tell them you were first up the stairs?" he mocked.

"You and your fucking sidekick attacked me," she said.

Ivan laughed again. With more than just a hint of disdain in his voice, he told her that he was going for a drink and, when she came to her senses, she was welcome to join him.

Sarah watched with her hand on the chair as she tried to regain her balance. He sauntered out of the room without another word to her. The sound of that metallic click as the door closed would be one she would never forget.

She slumped onto the seat and grimaced from an internal pain. She had been gripping the chair for what seemed like an age. Her hands were shaking, and she felt cold. The pain was beginning to ease. After a few moments, that felt like hours, she slowly rose to her feet. She tried to straighten her hair and wipe away her smeared lipstick. She pulled down her blouse and tried to remove some of the creases. She then turned and, with a deliberate but feigned poise, she took a few steps to the door.

She stepped out into the landing and inched her way to the top of the stairs and stopped. There was more pain and a lot of spasms were hitting her. They seemed to wash over her like a boat swallowed by a gigantic wave. It was then that she realised there was blood running down her inner thighs.

She gripped the banister with her left hand but was feeling light-headed. She wobbled at the top of the staircase and started to fall. In a flash, Luca caught her without a second to spare.

"Oh, mother of mercy," he cried, as Sarah collapsed into his protective arms.

Thirty-five minutes later, Sarah was admitted to the Accident and Emergency Department of Nailton Hospital, having been assessed by a Police Examiner. The doctor inserted three stitches into her perineum, which was ripped, and prescribed a course of antibiotics. When her blood pressure dropped back to an acceptable level, she was discharged with orders to return the next day for further checks to be made. Her mother and stepfather had responded to a call from the hospital admissions desk and were together in the waiting room wanting to take her home. As the maternal arms wrapped around her, Sarah whispered into her mother's ear: "Mum, they fucking raped me!"

Back at Heaton Van Sales, the party had come to abrupt end after the ambulance had taken Sarah to hospital. The gossip-mill was turning fast. The police questioned everyone present and recorded their full names and contact details before they were allowed to leave.

The Detective Inspector had arrived and his team had surveyed and catalogued the chaotic remnants of the party: food trodden into the floor; bins overflowing with empty beer cans, wine and spirit bottles; and the pungent smell of stale alcohol that hung in the air like an odious fog. Those who had partaken in other party accessories were paranoid beyond belief and probably brought more unwanted attention upon themselves by their furtive, twitching faces. The police were not interested in that aspect. They concentrated their investigations on the initial questioning of Ivan, Ethan and Luca. All the members of the reception desk were keen to make statements. At around eleven o'clock the Detective Inspector cautioned Ivan and Ethan and arrested them on suspicion of aggravated assault and rape.

There was only one topic of conversation throughout the office on Monday. Sarah did not report for work and Ivan and Ethan were missing. Craig was furious in having to have spent a lot of time dealing with Yvette, the personnel director, over the weekend. She laid out the factual and legal position to the chairman and notified Ivan and Ethan that they were suspended, pending the outcome of the police inquiry together with an internal company investigation. Craig was mainly concerned with the costs involved and whether the incident could depress sales.

Some weeks later, Amanda Buckingham was feeling the lump in Rumpole's belly. She felt awful. She'd always been diligent about getting him checked out when he had been ill but, this time, engrossed in her work and thoughts, she kept forgetting to book an appointment.

An hour later, the on-duty vet was ruffling Rumpole's head. Amanda's stomach turned; *one phone call was all I needed to have made so why did it take me so long to do it!* Her pet licked the vet's hand.

"I've been so irresponsible," said Amanda.

"No, not at all, don't be too hard on yourself," replied the vet, Ben Lister. Ben smiled at her reassuringly and made eye contact. Amanda held his gaze for several moments and then he broke away with an over-elaborate, "Anyway...back to Rumpole."

She had met him on several occasions when taking the cat for his injections and regular check-ups. Ben often teased Amanda with the suggestion that she should receive a loyalty card for the number of visits she accumulated in a year. Rumpole was nine years old which, in human terms, was around sixty-five years.

The vet's good looks were not lost on Amanda – and nor were hers on him. He had, at one of their earlier encounters, nodded with respect and interest when Amanda dropped into conversation that she was a barrister. Since then he teased her about her profession and told her the name for the cat was cute but a little obvious.

Amanda seldom missed signals. She was trained to read people and was blessed with an above average gift of intuition. For once, she merely took Ben's interest as part of the bedside manner. She later made a conscious effort to pay more attention to Ben's non-cat chat.

The vet was studying a scan of the lump in Rumpole's stomach. Amanda caught his gaze. He looked up.

"Yes, it's as I thought," and, with a slight pause for dramatic effect as Amanda held her breath, continued, "it's a cat."

He smiled and Amanda laughed.

"It's not too critical," he diagnosed, after a moment or so of careful deliberation.

"Too?" was the word that Amanda heard and repeated.

Perhaps, somewhat unprofessionally, he walked over to her and put his arm around her shoulders; it seemed, somehow, acceptable. She felt him squeeze her.

"You say he's had no food since late last night, so we'll take the lump out later today," he said, "and then, I'm afraid, it's in the hands of Saint Gertrude." He smiled at Amanda who seemed bemused. "Saint Gertrude is the patron saint of cats," he added.

"If it's cancer?" she asked.

"We'll send the lump for biopsy, and we'll find that out later. The first priority is to remove the growth and get him stable and comfortable," said Ben.

"What are his chances?" she asked.

"If Ben Lister is operating, better than most," quipped the vet.

Amanda appreciated the further effort at light-heartedness. Ben put Rumpole into his cage and he buzzed for a nurse to take him away.

"You go off and win your case and I'll fight on here," he suggested. "I'll text you when I have some news." He stared at her. "We'll do our best for him," he said.

"You and Saint Gertrude," said Amanda.

From her early days as a barrister, the Head of Hartington Chambers, located in Lincoln's Inn in central London, had taken a special interest in the niece of his friend, Anthony Buckingham.

As Amanda was sitting directly in front of Rufus Hetherington-Jones QC, she was being circumspect in reflecting her annoyance.

"Firstly, Rufus, I defend – so why have I received a prosecution brief?" she asked.

"We take what we're given," responded the Head of Chambers. "You know that is the way it works." He then repeated his favourite adage. "You know what I always say, Amanda: 'It is better to have your hand up than out'."

Nodding impatiently, Amanda continued her objections.

"Secondly, and after my review of the papers, I understand why the CPS is bringing this case to court, but I've got some concerns. I am not sure how I can convince a jury that she did not consent. She led the way to the boardroom. She allowed sex to take place with the first man and, although she claims she said "No", she still had sex with the second one. She cannot explain why she allowed this man to remain in the room at the beginning or why she did not protest when the door was locked. She must have realised that they intended to have sex with her." She raised her eyebrows as she awaited Rufus' reply.

Amanda was taking out her frustration, at the brief she had been presented with, on her Head of Chambers. This was not usually a wise course of action for any barrister at Hartington to follow. However, given the nature of their relationship, she was allowed a certain degree of latitude which was not afforded to any of her peers – and most certainly not to her colleague, with whom she shared a room, Mr Trevor Hamper-Houghton.

As the two barristers continued to debate the case, the usual hum of activity, in and around the Clerk's room, was beginning to wane as other members of Chambers and staff were passively listening to the conversation while trying to appear, and in the most failing, to look busy. They were enjoying the verbal back and forth as the barristers traded shots in a game of intellectual tennis.

Rufus, noting that they were becoming a distraction, waved Amanda into one of empty conference rooms. As he did so he caught the eye of Hartington Chambers' practice manager, a seasoned clerk by the name of David Blyth. David was a 'Dave' from Essex who had clerked his way up the ranks and, whilst he called himself Dave, Rufus always referred to him as David.

Rufus had no problem talking through any issue with anyone at chambers and he liked the paternal persona he thought he cultivated. Not all, if any, agreed that he generated this very well. However, no-one ever told him and so Rufus's belief in his own 'father-figure' status remained a constant source of amusement within chambers and no more so than to Dave and the rest of the support staff.

Amanda dutifully followed him into the conference room. Rufus closed the door. She sat down without waiting to be asked as she could feel her inner tension mounting. She decided to speak first.

"Rufus, let me summarise the position." She lingered for a second or so, allowing Rufus to take a seat opposite her, and so she could re-gather her momentum lost by the change of scenery. "Sarah Tomkins was one of the leaders in organising the office party. She had, by her own admission, drunk a lot of alcohol. There were drugs on hand but there is no suggestion that she used them. She went willingly with Ivan, and his associate Ethan Delaney, to the boardroom away from the party. She, in her own statement, claimed she protested that Ethan was there but, nevertheless, had consensual intercourse with Ivan. Her clothes were ripped but there is nothing to suggest she resisted at that point."

Rufus leant into the middle of the table and opened a bottle of expensive bottled water. He poured himself and Amanda a glass each. He then sat back, awaiting the next volley.

Amanda nodded her thanks. Moving the glass in front of her, she didn't wait for a coaster – much to the annoyance of Rufus. She carried on.

"Now, this is where matters get even more complicated. Ethan alleges he was encouraged by Sarah to have sex with her; she says she said "No". Sarah then claimed that someone hit her on the side of her head, but the Police Examiner reported no bruising. Sex occurred, the accused say, with consent, Sarah says the opposite."

Rufus, having had little to say so far, finished his glass of water with an audible smack of his lips. Sarah moved on, ignoring the noise.

"The two men then abandoned her and return to the party. Sarah found her own way out of the room, discovered she was bleeding, and collapsed. Luckily, Luca Toskas caught her. She was taken to hospital where she had three stitches to her perineum and was prescribed antibiotics."

She hesitated momentarily and looked down at her notes.

"Ivan was charged with sexual assault and Ethan with sexual assault and rape. I gather that the CPS considered charging Ivan with rape as well, but they subsequently dropped that charge against him because there was not sufficient evidence."

Amanda drained her glass, this time placing it neatly in the centre of her coaster. She looked at Rufus. He returned eye contact and Amanda concluded with, "They are both, without a doubt, guilty."

"So, prove it and get a conviction," said the Head of Hartington Chambers in a rather matter-of-fact tone.

"I can't prove either of the charges and the defence counsel will slaughter Sarah in the witness box."

"And you lose a case," interjected Rufus.

"I can live with that, Rufus, but I don't want the see the woman destroyed."

Carefully, and with a degree of sensitivity, he responded.

"Right, Amanda, let's take a step back and focus on what you have in your favour?"

Amanda snapped, "You mean in Sarah's favour, surely!"

Rufus recoiled back in his chair, with his arms out in front of him, in surrender.

He did not understand what Amanda said next because it was mumbled and certainly not in English.

With a slight air of apology, she smiled.

"Sorry, Rufus. Cantonese."

It broke the tension. Laughing in reply, Rufus added, "I can speak French."

"Eh bien," countered Amanda.

The two barristers sat silently for a moment until Amanda declared, "I can certainly present enough evidence, but it is about how the jury view Ivan and Edward. Ivan is a father and has a pregnant partner. Ethan, from the statements on file, is the more aggressive personality but they both maintain that sex with Sarah was consensual."

"The CPS is bringing the case, not you, Amanda," declared Rufus, "and you cannot get emotionally involved." He wondered if he was being too cold-hearted and tried to back-track. "The CPS is to lead and prepare the evidence and your job is to present it in the best way and then allow the jury to decide the outcome."

That was the end of the conversation, Amanda was not really sure if the discussion had been of any use, but she was grateful Rufus had at least listened to her. She followed him to the door and, as he politely ushered her out of the conference room, her mobile phone vibrated.

She walked a few paces and then read the message. *'Op in 30 mins. R is peaceful. B.'*

Amanda sat with the CPS officer and went through the police files, the evidence and the charges. They had a lot of work to do. Inwardly, Amanda lacked confidence in the case, but the CPS was optimistically bullish. While they waited for Sarah Tomkins to arrive, Amanda decided to express her reservations. The CPS solicitor was indifferent. "We have passed the threshold test," was the 'stock' response. Amanda raised her concerns from a professional standpoint; personally, she felt a sense of unease and impending defeat.

Sarah Tomkins arrived and was ushered into the meeting room by a male caseworker, perhaps in his early twenties who, incredibly, 'checked out' Sarah's behind as he closed the door. Amanda noticed this with a sense of utter incredulity that she only just managed to keep to herself. It was with a heavy heart that she smiled at Sarah as she sat down at the table.

She was wearing a blue top, pressed jeans, sandals and her hair was cut short.

"I'm here, Sarah, to understand your position and to prepare the Crown's case," she began.

"Thank you," interjected Sarah, "but, please, no legal niceties; there is no need."

"OK," she replied. She waited as Sarah rummaged in her bag. She put two pieces of menthol chewing gum into her mouth and began to chew. Amanda understood that this was her signal to press on and go to work.

The meeting lasted for several hours. Sarah was composed throughout and responded honestly to Amanda's detailed questions. The CPS solicitor added much to the conversation about how Sarah would give her evidence at the forthcoming trial. Sarah and the CPS solicitor had discussed and agreed that she would not seek any special measures in relation to the giving of evidence. Amanda was impressed with the courageous approach being taken by Sarah.

After the meeting ended, and on her journey back to Chambers, she reflected on what Sarah had said. The conclusion was the same as it had been earlier in the day: this case was going to test the barrister to the limits of her abilities.

Later that afternoon, Amanda was in her office, poring over the case file and her notes from the meeting. Papers were strewn across the table, on the floor and on the windowsill behind her. Post-it notes of all shapes, sizes and colours protruded from all angles making, to the untrained eye, her desk seem like a primary school art collage. Amanda felt comforted by the effort she was putting in and she gained some reassurance that, at the very least, she was going to be well prepared for trial.

She sensed her mobile phone vibrate on her desk. Searching through papers and bundles and textbooks she finally located it hidden between the pages of her notepad.

She read the message received:

'Op over. R rather poorly. Sorry. B.'

She read the message again. She drafted a response but didn't send it. She placed her mobile into her bag and returned to her paperwork.

Amanda spent Sunday afternoon with Trevor Hamper-Houghton. He was courteous, funny and well-informed. He asked her for another 'pre-date date' as he liked to call their irregular gatherings. She agreed to meet him again the following Saturday and he suggested taking the Eurostar to Brussels for a day trip. She wondered if she had shown him sufficient enthusiasm as he clumsily backtracked in fear of being rejected.

The truth of the matter was that Amanda's mind was preoccupied with the upcoming case. Her pre-occupation with Sarah's innocence continued to invade her rather cramped brain. The preliminary hearing was set for Monday. If the defendants didn't have a Road to Damascus bout of conscience, the matter would be listed for trial at Crown Court.

Monday came and went. The two defendants confirmed their respective names and their pleas of 'not guilty'. Sarah was not present. This entire episode lasted a matter of minutes and was, at best, perfunctory.

Amanda had her routines as well as her quirks. On the morning of each new trial she did two things. She rose early and went to the gym. Her personal trainer, Zach, was quite amenable to this routine as Amanda was paying well over the odds. Although he kept his thoughts to himself, he relished the look of Amanda in Lycra kit. She liked to box before a trial; pad work, mainly, but she found it far more rewarding than a normal gym session. The second of her pre-trial rituals was a real indulgence. It was a full-fat cappuccino with chocolate sprinkles from her favourite coffee shop just off Lincoln's Inn Square.

She sat in her room at Chambers, a dank, mouldy old pump room in the bowels of the Old Square. The clerks had told her it was only a temporary office but that had been several years ago. Energised by her gym work-out and a warm feeling inside as she devoured her cappuccino extravaganza, Amanda was ready.

With a clenched fist of delight as she three-pointed her immaculately drained take-away cup into the wastepaper bin, Amanda picked up her trolley bag that she had carefully packed. The handle was grabbed and, with a hefty tug, given the weight of the paper inside, she strode away. Amanda walked assertively passed the other 'temporary' residents of her floor. Her office door had closed with a thud and inside it was now almost completely dark, save for the neon glow of the phone that had been left on her desk.

A few moments later, Amanda re-entered her office and grabbed her mobile, stuffing it into her coat pocket. She then left for a second time, with a renewed determination to win the case.

Nailton Crown Court was as inspiring as a Stalinist gulag in the depths of winter. It lacked warmth, charm and architectural appeal. "Buildings can be warm and inviting," thought Amanda, but this court edifice was neither, especially as the heating was unreliable.

In the robing room, Amanda donned her black gown and short wig. It wasn't a flattering look for anyone, but she quite liked the history and the tradition behind it. Walking into court, with a bow of the head as she entered, she took her place next to her trolley bag. Meticulously she laid out her papers, notes and pens. She poured herself a beaker full of tepid tap water that had been placed in a plastic jug by the court clerk.

There was nothing else she needed to do. She was ready. She was Amanda Buckingham, prosecution counsel.

Unlike scenes from Hollywood movies, British jury selection consists of a series of random ballots. First you are summoned, then you are allocated an alpha-numeric reference and placed into a pool. Fifteen of your pool colleagues then attend before the judge and the court where a final lottery takes place. If your number comes up, you take one of the twelve seats. It's like a bizarre game of musical chairs, without music, levity or a prize, pondered Amanda. She, even as a junior member of Chambers, had seen too many jury formations to easily recall each in detail but, every time, the sheer randomness never disappointed her. She was not a football fan but, as she watched the jurors-in-waiting being called as jurors, and taking their seats in two banks of six, Amanda likened the process to those halcyon days of cup draws with stiff, crusty old farts pulling numbered balls out of silk bags.

Assessing the final twelve members of the jury was an essential element of the criminal legal process, whether you are defending or prosecuting. Amanda hoped that she would be fortunate with the final make-up. Inwardly, she prayed for more women than men to be on the jury. She reasoned that women would be more empathetic towards Sarah.

The final composition of the jury was six men and six women.

"It could have been worse," she said to herself.

Judge Clarke went through his usual repartee. He was a solid and well-respected man, but he had certain peccadilloes. Amanda had been before him on several previous occasions. While he would never tolerate questioning off the beaten path, he had always allowed her some degree of latitude. Judge Clarke reminded the jury of their serious and civic duties in painstaking detail. Some of the jury were already lost; others took frantic notes; one looked half-asleep. When he had finished with the jury he turned to public gallery.

Amanda sat watching the jury, looking for eye contact. She caught two or three sets of eyes and smiled back – not a teeth flasher, but a professional smile with a slight nod.

Sarah's mother and stepfather sat quietly together in the gallery. They were surrounded by friends of the defendants and a few unknowns who were looking for some enthralling courtroom jousting. There was a law student present – he was obviously a student as his legal textbooks were by his side together with a cheap-looking packet sandwich.

The only other person left in the room was Archie Morton, an experienced bulldog of a defence counsel. He had made a good living in defending criminal cases; his motto (and that of Waitland Chambers where he had practised and honed his craft for two decades) was, '*If they pay, we'll plead nay*'.

Amanda really didn't like him at all, even on a professional level. He was fixated by money and the

'Holy Grail' of becoming a QC. There was no altruism, no public interest, no soul to Archie Morton; this did, however, make him a formidable opponent and Amanda knew she would have to be at the top of her game from the off.

During a long and tedious narrative from Judge Clarke, Archie did nothing other than assess and scan the jury. He was slick, like slow-moving oil, and just as toxic, but for some reason, he often managed to get jury members on his side. He nodded to some, smiled at others and stared others out.

All of this administration and ground rules meant that Judge Clarke decided on an early lunch; the jury looked relieved and funnelled out of the courtroom. The two defendants seemed confused at this unexpected halt in proceedings. Eventually, the court room emptied save for Archie and Amanda.

"Well then, Buckers," sneered Morton, "I see you are playing with the other side of the bat on this one." He continued the cricket analogies. "The wicket's no good for you, I'm afraid, and there's no chance of this going five days."

Amanda didn't follow cricket and so Morton's words were lost on her. She had to respond, albeit ineffectively.

"I'm happy to take this one on," she stammered.

She finished packing away her papers into her trolley bag and left the courtroom.

After an uninspiring lunch with the CPS solicitor, Amanda opened the Crown's case against Mr Ivan Derbyshire and Mr Edward Delaney. Every single word had been revised, reviewed, amended, modified and triple checked. Amanda delivered her speech perfectly. Her tone was spot on and the tempo was even better. Silence is such a powerful tool in any successful advocate's arsenal and Amanda let every detail of the events that had taken place in the Heaton Van Sales boardroom hang in the air like poisoned arrows. There was a deathly silence as they landed on the jury.

Archie, however, had seen this coming. By the time he'd dissected Amanda's opening comments, the visitor in the gallery was perplexed. What would the verdict be? At the end of day one, the law student summarised his notes with two words: Not Guilty.

Day two saw the start of witness evidence. The first person called took the oath and confirmed that his name was Luca Gabor Toskas. He stated that his parents had brought him and his sister to live in the United Kingdom in the 1990s. He said that he had joined Heaton Van Sales three years ago and was part of Ivan's team. Luca made it clear that he liked his job very much.

He then went through the events of the Friday evening, when the alleged assault took place, and confirmed that he had followed Ivan, Ethan and Sarah up the stairs. Ivan had told him to go back to the party. He said that he did not mind because a pretty blonde girl was waiting for him.

He categorically denied taking any drugs but confirmed that they were available but the source of such were unknown to him.

"So, Mr Toskas, how far up the stairs did you climb?" asked Amanda.

"To the first floor," he replied.

"And that was the point when Mr Derbyshire told you to return to the party."

"Yes."

"What did he say?" asked Amanda.

"He made it clear that I was not welcome," replied Luca.

"What words did he use, Mr Toskas?"

The assistant salesman looked around him, unsure if he was allowed to swear an oath and in court. Amanda read the situation and placated the witness with a smile.

"He told me to piss off," he stuttered.

There was a snigger around the court room. Judge Clarke raised one of his bushy eyebrows in annoyance and gently tapped his bench with his left-hand knuckles to let everyone know he had heard the laughter and that it was not permitted in *his* court.

Amanda repeated, "'Piss off'…do you think that is a friendly way to be spoken to, Mr Toskas?"

"It's the way he always speaks to me," he replied.

"I can imagine," she acknowledged, glancing at Judge Clarke. He'd heard her comment, but, thankfully, let it slide. Archie was texting under the table, so he missed her unprofessional remark.

Amanda noticed that two of the six women who made up the jury were fidgeting and exchanging nods of agreement.

"Did you immediately return to the party?" enquired Amanda.

"Yes. You can be sure. I'm olive-skinned. The girls love us Europeans."

There was at least one laugh from the gallery. The student looked around, but all heads had dropped like a mass prayer had been called. Judge Clarke imperiously scowled at where the noise had come from. Waiting for the nod from the judge, Amanda stood still. The approval came and she began again.

"So, you returned to the party?"

"Yes."

"Therefore, you have no idea what happened to Mr Derbyshire, Mr Delaney and Miss Tomkins," countered Amanda.

"We all know what happened," said Luca.

"How do you know?" pounced Amanda.

"Well...I don't. I wasn't there," stammered Luca.

"Thank you, Mr Toskas," interrupted Amanda, "we have your evidence that you were not there. Now, I want to ask you about the events that happened later. This was when Miss Tomkins collapsed into your arms. This took place on the third floor?"

"At the bottom of the stairs leading up to the boardroom," Luca said.

"On the third floor," said Amanda.

"Yes."

"What were you doing there?" she asked.

"I have explained. Ivan and Ethan are my friends. I wanted to make sure they were having fun."

The courtroom fell into a brief period of silence as Amanda waited for Luca to keep talking. After a few moments it was apparent that he would not; Amanda then rallied.

"So, what about the girl at the party?" asked Amanda.

"I don't understand you," said Luca.

Amanda debated explaining the point, but she hesitated.

"You went up the stairs and you caught Miss Tomkins."

"Yes. There was blood on her hand."

"Yes, thank you, Mr Toskas. We will come to that

shortly," declared Amanda. She paused and wrote that down on her notepad.

"You must have passed Mr Derbyshire and Mr Delaney on their way down the stairs then?" Amanda asked.

"Just Ivan," he said. "We passed as he went back into the party."

Luca ran his hand through his hair and fiddled with his tie. He went for the water and gulped down a large cup full.

"Mr Delaney was upstairs," stated Amanda.

Morton had finished his texting and he rose to his feet.

"It would seem, Your Honour, that this is a statement of conjecture rather than a question," said the defence counsel.

"Miss Buckingham?" queried Judge Clarke. He had that judicial knack of saying the same words on multiple occasions but each time they sounded and meant something entirely different.

Amanda turned back to the witness box. Smiling, she said, "You owe a lot to your two friends, don't you, Mr Toskas?"

"I have a great job, thanks to Ivan and Ethan," said Luca.

"Would I be right in thinking you'd do anything for them?" asked Amanda.

Archie was up like a rocket. "Your Honour!" he screeched.

Amanda said flatly, "No further questions" and sat down.

The defence counsel stared at Amanda. He shuffled his feet, pulled on the lapels of his gown and began his questioning.

"Mr Toskas, hello. I'm Mr Archie Morton and I want to ask you just one question."

Luca smiled as he hoped he'd soon to be out of the witness box.

"When you left Mr Derbyshire, Mr Delaney and Miss Tomkins to go further up the stairs, at the point when Mr Derbyshire told you to go back to the party, what was your impression about Miss Tomkins' attitude?"

"I do not understand the question," said Luca.

"Was it your impression that Miss Tomkins was going willingly with the two men?" rephrased the defence counsel.

"She was laughing and touching Ivan," he answered. "She was going up the stairs quite quickly; I know that because I was taking two steps at a time myself."

"No further questions," declared Archie as he sat down with a smugness that some barristers possess.

Amanda's re-examination was cursory. She knew that she had misjudged Luca and had, naively, not seen Archie's single question coming until it was too late.

Judge Clarke decided on an early finish. The jury were delighted until he kept everyone another ten minutes to explain that the members of the jury must not talk to anyone about the case or undertake any research in relation to the facts or the law.

As Amanda watched the two defendants depart, she was repulsed by the thumbs up Ethan Delaney gave to Archie. She spoke to the CPS solicitor outside the courtroom and, after a few perfunctory comments, they agreed that it was early days. She left the building through a side exit and switched on her mobile phone.

There were three messages and several emails, but

she knew the one she would open first. She read the words carefully:

'R has an infection. On antibiotics. Not good. Lump was benign. B.'

Tuesday was a damp, mild June day. It started badly for the prosecution team and never recovered. Edward Delaney entered the witness box and promised to tell the truth. He radiated self-confidence. He agreed with everything that Amanda asked him.

Yes, he had gone up to the boardroom to have sex with Sarah. None of them had taken drugs although all three had consumed rather a lot of alcohol: in his case, he estimated seven cans of lager.

He confirmed that he was in awe of Ivan and would do anything for him. He liked Luca, and he thought that Sarah was "sensational". He did not deny that he had made a rather crude suggestion involving the two males but said that Sarah had applauded his idea. Amanda glanced to her left; Sarah was shaking her head in silent outrage.

She had chosen to attend the trial, and, at the pre-trial conference with the CPS, she agreed that she would not opt for any of the evidential special measures that were afforded to victims of sexual assaults. Sarah had also waived her right to give evidence by video-link even though the CPS solicitor had delicately explained that she might find being questioned in the witness box incredibly harrowing. Ultimately the CPS made the ruling, but Sarah confirmed it was the right thing to do. It was a courageous decision.

Amanda continued with her questioning of Ethan.

"Mr Delaney, I regret that I need to raise an

unpleasant matter with you."

Ethan Delaney remained impassive.

"Do you deny that, at the end of your assault on..."

"If I may, Your Honour," cried out Archie Morton, "counsel is prejudging the decision of the jury. Her statement is grossly misleading."

Judge Clarke was displeased. He decided to reassert his authority.

"Miss Buckingham! I will not allow you any further leeway in this case. You will not again, in my court, make such a distorted statement." He turned to the jury and ordered them to disregard the question.

Amanda was stung by the judicial rebuke.

"I apologise, Your Honour," she said, sensing that she might have lost the momentum that she was carefully trying to build.

"Mr Delaney," she continued. "Did you, towards the end of the events in question, touch Miss Tomkins' inner thighs?"

"No," Delaney replied.

"No, Mr Delaney?" exclaimed Amanda incredulously. "May I remind you that you are under oath and you are required to tell the truth."

"I did not force myself on Sarah. She was gagging for it and she encouraged me." He paused and added, "She was laughing. She loved it."

There was total silence in the courtroom. Sarah Tomkins collapsed in tears into her mothers' arms. The judge allowed a few moments to elapse before indicating to Amanda that she should continue.

"What happened next?"

"I was wondering whether we might do other things," responded the witness.

"Other things?" asked Amanda.

"Well, she was having fun."

Sarah Tomkins put her hands over her face and wept silently.

Judge Clarke was not an uncaring or insensitive man. Realising that the emotions inside his courtroom had ratcheted up, and the increased tension had engulfed everyone like a noxious gas, he called a halt to proceedings and ordered that everyone would take an early lunch. He then asked both barristers into his Chambers. This style of judicial conference used to be quite commonplace but, with the various changes to legal processes, they now occur less often. When they do take place, what is said is added to the Digital Audio Recording Transcription and Storage court recording system – DARTS. Judge Clarke was careful in what he said to both barristers, but he made it abundantly clear that he was growing displeased with their conduct. Both Amanda and Archie left, chastened, like two naughty schoolchildren exiting the headmaster's office.

When the court resumed, Archie Morton revisited all the previous evidence and managed to convey to Amanda and, in her view, the jury as well, Ethan Delaney's disbelief that Sarah was suggesting she had not participated willingly. By the end of the day's proceedings, the body language of several of the jury appeared to suggest that they were satisfied that the accused might be innocent.

The records of the police examiner were admitted without objection from either barrister so the third witness to take the stand was Dr Rebecca Atkinson.

Amanda took a line of questioning that proved to be a little too casual. She established that Dr Atkinson had been on duty at the Accident and Emergency Department of Nailton Hospital on the Friday night when the Heaton party had taken place. Dr Atkinson confirmed that she had examined the patient identified as Sarah Tomkins and had inserted three stitches inside her perineum. She had prescribed a course of antibiotics and later discharged the patient as they were desperately short of beds.

When asked the direct and final question, Dr Atkinson said that, in her medical opinion, the injuries, which included redness on the inner thighs, were consistent with a physical sexual assault.

Amanda left the last phrase hanging in the air and invited her professional adversary to cross-examine the witness.

Archie Morton rose to his feet slowly and with deliberate purpose.

"Dr Atkinson," he began. "How long was it between Sarah Tomkins arriving at the Accident and Emergency Department and your examination taking place?"

"I can't be certain," replied the doctor. "We were very busy that evening. There had been a fire in the town centre, and we had some patients needing help with breathing difficulties due to smoke inhalation."

"Quite," observed the weasel-like barrister. "Thank you for your helpful answer, Dr Atkinson. We accept the pressures you must face in your work. I will repeat my question. How long was it between Sarah Tomkins…?"

"I understand the question," snapped the doctor. "I think from memory it was about three hours which is within the government's target timings."

"Three hours," repeated the defence counsel. "Can we therefore conclude that the injuries sustained by Sarah Tomkins were not considered to be an emergency?"

"No," responded the doctor. "I work in the Emergency Department."

"You work, Dr Atkinson, in the Accident and Emergency Department. I put it to you that the injuries sustained by Sarah Tomkins were not an emergency. They were an accident, which you correctly and efficiently treated."

"She needed stitches," said the doctor. "She had been assaulted."

"We'll come on to that," said Archie. "If you had not seen Sarah Tomkins for four hours, what would have been the medical consequences?"

"She needed stitches," replied Rebecca. "She had been assaulted."

"Dr Atkinson, it is not for you to say she had been assaulted." Archie paused to allow the jury to consider his words. "Shall we agree," he continued "that your patient was not an emergency? She needed hospital treatment which was non-urgent?"

"You're putting words in my mouth," replied Dr Atkinson.

Amanda was now realising that she had erred badly in not taking the doctor's evidence more seriously and that there should have been a lot more direct questioning as to the nature and extent of Sarah's injuries. On several occasions she went to challenge Archie Morton's questions but decided to wait.

"You have said that you inserted three stitches, Dr Atkinson. Where was that?"

"The perineum, at the entry of the vagina."

"How long is the vagina?" asked Archie Morton.

"It varies but shall we say about four inches in this patient's case."

"And where, Dr Atkinson, were the stitches inserted. How deep in did you have to go?" asked Archie.

"I inserted the injuries at the opening," replied the doctor.

"The opening," mused the defence counsel. "And why did you insert three stitches?"

"Your Honour," pleaded Amanda "There is simply no purpose in this line of questioning. We have accepted that Sarah Tomkins required three stitches."

"I'll permit the question," said Judge Clarke.

"Thank you, Your Honour." Archie Morton took a pace back and stared at the witness.

"Could Sarah Tomkins have managed with two stitches?" he asked.

"In my medical opinion..."

"Did the injury need stitches at all?" he said. "Was there internal bleeding?"

"There was no bleeding. There was a tear which, in my medical opinion, required stitches."

"Would you have endangered the patient if you had inserted two stitches?" asked Archie.

"In my medical opinion..."

"Thank you, Doctor Atkinson. How often do you come across this type of injury?"

"More often than you might imagine," said Dr Atkinson.

"Are you able to explain to the court the usual cause?" asked Archie.

"Oh. That's easy. The vagina is quite delicate and nearly always it's the result of physical intercourse taking place. It looks worse..."

The defence counsel was quite happy for the doctor to continue talking.

"...because injuries in what is a very sensitive area can bleed a lot during and after sex, due to the heart working harder."

"The result of sexual intercourse, Dr Atkinson. Between a man and a woman."

"Well, there are a number of variations but yes, heterosexual sex."

"Dr Atkinson. You have referred to Sarah Tomkins being assaulted. You witnessed the alleged assault, did you?"

"Of course not. The paramedics told us. It was written on her triage notes. It's also what the patient had told them."

"The injury you treated. Can you say with any certainty how it was caused?"

"It was consistent with a physical assault."

"Or was it consistent with normal consensual sexual intercourse?" asked Archie.

"Well, I suppose it could have been."

"Can you say, Dr Atkinson, with any degree of certainty, that, in your opinion, there was clear evidence that your patient had been physically assaulted?"

The witness hesitated.

Archie Morton stood, his eyes fixed on the witness stand and counted to ten in his head.

"Dr Atkinson," he continued. "Did your patient, Sarah Tomkins, tell you that she had been assaulted?"

"She didn't say very much at all and I had a heavy workload."

"I want to repeat your words, Dr Atkinson," said Archie. "'She didn't say very much'." Does that tell you anything?"

"Women who have been sexually assaulted usually react in one of two ways," replied the doctor. "Some, quite evidently, are distressed and traumatised. Others say absolutely nothing."

"And what does the reaction tell you?" asked Archie.

"Usually I'm afraid that I'm too busy tending to the medical needs of my patients to get too involved in their mental state." She paused. "If I feel a patient needs psychiatric support, I will call in a colleague."

"Thank you, Dr Atkinson," smiled Archie. "What you are telling the ladies and gentlemen of the jury is that you were otherwise engaged with your medical duties and, in truth, you had little idea about Sarah Tomkins' emotional state."

"I wouldn't put it like that," replied the doctor.

"I want to ask you about the alleged damaged skin on her inner thighs," continued Archie. "What treatment did you administer? How many marks were there?" he asked.

"The skin was inflamed and red," said the doctor.

"And how many marks were there?"

"There were several impressions on the skin. They did not need treating although I did rub some cream into her body to help the healing."

Archie continued his questioning.

"Dr Atkinson. I only have two more questions for you. The redness, as you call it, on Sarah Tomkins's thighs. If that had been her only injury, how would you have treated it?"

"I have no way of knowing that," replied the witness. "She would never have reached me. A nurse would have seen her."

"Thank you," said Archie. "My final question. Can you please describe the condition of Sarah Tomkins when you first examined her?"

"She was lying on the bed. She was half asleep."

"When you talked to her, was she rational?"

"She asked if she could still have children."

"What was your answer, Dr Atkinson?"

"I was able to tell her that, as far as I could be certain, she was physically fine, but she should see her own doctor if she wanted further reassurance."

"And you judged that physically, and emotionally, she was ready to be discharged after you had treated her?"

"Yes. We needed the bed."

"No further questions, Your Honour," said Archie Morton.

Amanda knew that it was too late to undo the damage inflicted by Archie Morton's incisive cross examination. She was personally affronted, but professional impressed, by Archie's skilful approach.

She watched again as Ethan Delaney put up his thumb towards Archie and the visitor's gallery. She vaguely heard Judge Clarke closing the day's proceedings and again advising the jury that they were not to talk to any third party about the case.

Amanda put her papers in her case and sat down to think. She had the option of re-examining Dr Atkinson in the morning, but she could see no advantage in doing this: there was little she could do now Archie had won the day. As she left the building, she turned on her mobile phone. There were seven messages and three missed calls. Not one of them was from Ben.

The law student's tally chart, with marks out of ten, from the back of the public gallery, now read: *Not Guilty 6. Guilty 3.* He needed to work on his mathematics.

Amanda left the court building in need of carbs. Arriving back at her flat via the local pizza takeaway, her mobile phone vibrated.

'So sorry. R is struggling. We're fighting for him. B.'

Amanda went into her bedroom, stripped off her clothes and put on her cheongsam. She returned to the kitchen and ate a thin and crispy Hawaiian pizza with extra pineapple as if she had not eaten for days. She managed all but a few crusts and one solitary slice which she threw into the bin. She collected a bottle of chilled mineral water from the fridge, and walked to the sofa, where she had discarded her case notes minutes earlier.

Later she went to bed before midnight but didn't fall sleep until after two in the morning. She then had a dream. She was back in Kowloon with Fat FrEthan or, rather, Fat Son Sue. He was telling her to work harder.

She made her first misjudgement on Wednesday morning by texting Trevor Hamper-Houghton to confirm their Saturday trip to Brussels. His curt reply of "Agreed" left her feeling a little emotionally empty.

Ivan Derbyshire proved to be a more challenging witness. He had clearly decided to say as little as possible and his repetition of "Yes" and "No" unsettled Amanda. He even prevaricated when giving the details of the deal he had secured for Heaton Van Sales and the commissions he had paid out of his bonus. In answer to the question "So you gave £200 to Sarah Tomkins?" he replied "Yes". When asked why he had done so, he said, "I wanted to".

Amanda took him through the events of the Friday evening: the party, the atmosphere, Sarah's disclosure that she suggested a more private party, the climb up the stairs, Ethan's role, his physicality, his shock at

Sarah's injuries about which he had known nothing, and his concern for her well-being.

Amanda played her trump card.

"Mr Derbyshire. You have a partner and you live together."

"Yes."

"You have a son?"

"Yes. Billy."

"I understand that your partner is pregnant."

"Yes."

"How many weeks?"

"Twenty something, I think."

"Was it difficult for you to explain to your partner that you had been unfaithful?"

Archie Morton went to object and then sat down again.

"No," said Derbyshire.

"No!" repeated Amanda. "What is her name?"

"Debbie."

"Debbie," said Amanda. "What does Debbie think about what's happened? How does she feel about you standing here before this court?"

Archie Morton again went to protest at the question but sat down.

"Nothing," said Ivan.

"Nothing," said Amanda.

Ivan remained quiet.

"You are asking the jury to believe that your pregnant partner was relaxed about you having sex with a work colleague."

"She told me to."

"I beg your pardon, Mr. Derbyshire. Are you saying that Debbie encouraged you to have sex with another woman?"

"Yes," he said. "With Sarah."

Amanda turned to Judge Clarke.

"Your Honour, this witness simply cannot be trusted with this evidence."

"Continue with your questions, please, Miss Buckingham," was the terse reply.

"Let me understand this exactly," said Amanda. "You are telling this court that your pregnant partner encouraged you to have sex with Sarah Tomkins?"

"Yes."

"Why?" asked Amanda.

"Debs is struggling. She's got high blood pressure. She understands that I need regular sex. She can't do it. She told me to shag Sarah. She worked at Heaton and said all the girls thought that Sarah was gagging for it."

The law student marked down another point for Not Guilty and then closed his notebook.

Amanda lay on her sofa in complete silence. There was no music, no background sound and no cat. She went over and over the evidence she had heard during the last three days. There was no doubt in her mind that Ivan and Ethan had assaulted Sarah Tomkins. Sarah's behaviour had muddied the waters by dancing with Ivan and wanting to have sex with Ivan. However, Sarah had never expected Ethan to become involved and immediately she made it clear that she was not consenting, the two salesmen had broken the law.

Sarah had been determined so far, but tomorrow she would give her testimony, and Archie would tear her to pieces.

Amanda was worried. She had never lost a case before, but she felt that might change tomorrow. She tried to sleep, she wanted it, she needed it but, as she drifted in and out of consciousness, she went back to her disagreement with the officer from the CPS.

"The decision to prosecute is quite straightforward, Miss Buckingham," she had said. "It's a clear case of assault and rape. The girl said "No". There was no consent. There were her injuries. There was the damage to her body. She collapsed down the stairs and was lucky that the man caught her. All you have to do is persuade the jury that Sarah is telling the truth, not the defendants."

Amanda tossed and turned from side to side. She put her arm out to rub Rumpole's head, but he was fighting for his life in the animal hospital.

In the early hours, Amanda woke from a fitful sleep and went over to the window. She looked at the lights of the twenty-four-hour city beneath her. She turned back to the divan and sat down with a glass of water in her hand.

Her memory went back to her abortion. The five-star treatment at the private hospital and Eileen's love and care, which partly mitigated the pain and humiliation. She relived the event. Even Fat FrEthan's judo training had not prepared her for a man of fifteen stones grabbing her from behind. He had seemed so caring and friendly. She accepted that they were moving towards the start of a relationship and she had arranged a doctor's appointment to ask for a prescription for birth control pills.

It was a sunny day and she drank too much wine. When his hand strayed too far up her thigh, she told him to stop and he complied. She relaxed and a few moments later stood up and removed her skirt and blouse to reveal her bikini. That was naively provocative. Five minutes later he came on her from behind. She collapsed under the pressure of his weight and was unable to stop him penetrating her. As they stood up and faced each other she suddenly executed a perfect *harai goshi*. The sweeping hip throw resulted in her assailant landing on his back with Amanda holding his arm which she was twisting against the joint.

"I am two inches away from breaking your shoulder," she said, before she released him and fled the scene.

What she did not do was to see the doctor and obtain a morning-after pill. It never occurred to her that she might be pregnant. She fought the increase in her weight until she started being sick in the mornings. Eileen knew immediately and booked an appointment for her to see a doctor at her own private clinic. Her uncle was not involved. She looked after her niece and rarely left her side. Her recovery from the termination was medically satisfactory and complete. Her aunt never once preached to her. She just hugged her.

The day before she was discharged from the hospital, she received a visitor. Anthony Buckingham, as always, looked immaculate. They discussed Tony Blair and the Conservative Party's inability to dislodge him. He moaned that his wife did not understand him and then winked at his niece.

He stood up to leave. As he reached the door he turned back.

"The chairman of a company," he began, "where I was marketing manager once saved my skin. I had dropped a huge clanger and he covered up for me. As I left his office after the biggest reprimand I had ever faced, he said to me, "Buckingham. Your gross incompetence is history. You judged the supplier on face value. You did not think things through. You did not check the facts. You can now only make one more error. If you fail to learn from your mistake, you'll leave us." He paused before choosing his words, "I did learn, and I prospered," he added.

As she stared at the closing door, Amanda made a vow to herself. She would learn from her mistakes. It was a lesson she was never to forget.

After she returned to her bed, she continued to slumber into the early hours. She inevitably thought further about Sarah Tomkins. She went over and over the events of the Heaton party. She wanted to be sure that she was not judging things on face value. At five-fifteen in the morning she received a text message and immediately pictured Rumpole alone in the animal hospital. She got out of bed and went into the lounge. She then read the brief request:

'Is it too early to chat? THH.'

She pressed his number and immediately heard his voice.

"Just wondered how your case was going?" he asked.

Amanda lay back on her bed and tried to avoid an adverse reaction from her friend because she was trying to look forward to their planned Saturday trip into Europe. It was not too long before Trevor was testing her. He explained that he had been in Chambers the previous afternoon (and he did not fail to mention that he had won a case against the Inland Revenue for one of their clients who had become involved in a dubious film financing scheme) and picked up comments that she was not handling the sexual assault too well. He then added to Amanda's angst by suggesting he might be able to advise her on her courtroom strategy.

Amanda proceeded to go through the key points of the case with him and was reassured that he did not interrupt or make any comment apart from the occasional "oh boy". When she had completed her summation, she admitted that she was nervous about putting Sarah Tomkins in the witness box.

"That's your big chance. Tell me about the jury," said Trevor.

Amanda went through the make-up: the six men and the six women.

"Pity," he concluded. "You need at least eight or nine women," he said.

"I know," admitted Amanda.

"Well, good luck. What approach will you be taking later?" he asked.

"I will try to show that she is a lovely woman who was assaulted. I shall focus on her evidence that she said "No"."

He interrupted her.

"Hang on, I want to top up my coffee."

Amanda used the interval to decide if their call was positive.

"Right. Back on duty," she heard him say. "Did you know that they call you 'AB' in the office? I'm going to call you 'AB'," he said. "Not very original I grant you, but it suits."

Did she just feel her heart race? For THH it was a rare moment of flirtatious banter.

"Well, BB," she said, "how would you handle Sarah?"

"BB?" he asked.

"Brilliant Barrister," she laughed.

"AB meets BB. Read all about it," he chuckled.

Amanda was enjoying their exchange. She really did wonder if THH might develop into something more real. Their similar legal backgrounds were a good start. She just wished he'd ask her more questions about herself.

"I would keep it short," he said. "You want the jury to be left with just one memory: she said "No"."

"And what about what Edward Delaney did to her?"

"I leave justice to the kingdom of heaven," said Trevor. "Good luck and let me know," and with that he terminated the call.

She went into the shower and turned the water to its hottest level. He was right. She realised that she was siding with Sarah and ignoring the facts. She knew that she only had one real opportunity to influence the jury. Sarah had said "No" and that is rape.

She dried herself and put on a tracksuit. She cycled on her machine for twenty minutes and felt awful. Her breakfast consisted of half a cup of filter coffee. Thursday was starting badly.

She re-read the message on her mobile phone:

'R very poorly. Trying different treatment. We're fighting for him. B.'

As she reached the court, she ran into Judge Clarke. He nodded and hurried on into his Chambers.

Later that morning, Sarah Tomkins strode confidently to the witness box, Amanda silently applauded her. She was wearing a demure grey suit, no make-up, a hair band and low heels.

195

At first, Amanda concentrated on her early career at Heaton Van Sales and her success in becoming head receptionist. When Sarah let slip that, last year, the company had allowed her time off to nurse her dying grandmother, Amanda was in like an Exocet missile. By the time she was finished, she had portrayed Sarah as a humane, selfless and caring person.

They covered the events of the Friday party, her willingness to have sex with Ivan and her initial enthusiasm as they climbed the stairs to the boardroom.

Amanda was heading for the key moment if she was to convince the jury of the defendants' guilt. She enabled Sarah to exhibit her utter horror when she realised that she was expected to have sex with a second man, her punitive treatment on the boardroom table and her repugnancy at the physical pain inflicted by Ethan.

"Miss Tomkins," said Amanda as she faced the jury. "Did you, or did you not, agree to have sex with Edward Delaney?"

"No, I did not," replied Sarah in a clear and confident voice.

"Did you use that word, 'No'? Is that what you said?"

"That is what I said both to Ivan and to Ethan. I said "No" and I meant no."

"No further questions," said Amanda, as she returned to her seat. She studied the faces of the jury members. She was convinced that she had sowed the seeds of doubt in several of their minds.

Whereupon Archie Morton rose to his feet with the deliberation of a man convinced of his own importance and he proceeded to attack the creditability of Sarah Tomkins.

"Your Honour, members of the jury, I must start my cross examination of this witness with an apology. My job is to defend my clients to the best of my humble abilities and is to prevent a possible miscarriage of justice. My two clients, Ivan Derbyshire and Edward Delaney, are two hard-working and successful businessmen who were seduced by a colleague at an office party. We, here today, are all worldly-wise and this type of liaison occurs up and down this great country of ours. So, all that is needed, members of the jury, is to deal with just one matter."

Amanda's instinct was telling her that the mother of all bombs was about to be detonated in the courtroom.

"Miss Tomkins," he exploded, "I wish I did not have to ask you this question." He paused with superb timing. "Do you regularly have sex with married men, or men who have longer-term partners?"

Sarah tried desperately to retain her dignity.

"I consider that an unfair question," she replied.

"Miss Tomkins," continued Archie Morton. "Do you have sex with men who effectively are cheating on another person?"

Amanda was on her feet but Judge Clarke took no notice and so she sat down.

"Ethan forced himself on me," she pleaded.

"Miss Tomkins, how many times have you had sex with a married or committed man?"

"Amanda was up on her feet. "Your Honour, this has nothing to do with this…" Her words were lost as Judge Clarke intervened

"The witness will please answer the question. Continue with your questions, Mr Morton."

"I'm obliged, Your Honour," he said. "Miss

Tomkins. Let's take this step by step." He smiled at the witness. "Can we assume that you usually know the marital status of the men with whom you have sex?"

"Yes," said Sarah in a hushed voice. "One or two pull the wool, but you usually know."

"And do you perform vigorous sexual acts in your relationships with the men with whom you choose to have a relationship?"

"Some men make demands, yes," said Sarah.

"And can we assume that you perform these acts willingly?"

"It is part of love-making," she said, as Amanda wanted the floor to open up and swallow her whole.

"Do men ever force themselves on you?" asked the defence counsel.

Amanda rose and held out her hands in exasperation.

Judge Clarke took off his glasses.

"Mr Morton. I must admit I am wondering if you are beginning to push my patience and that of this court."

"Thank you, Your Honour," he said as he nodded. He then paused with magnificent effect. "If Your Honour will allow me to reach my crucial question?"

"As quickly as you can, please Mr Morton," replied the judge.

"I am most grateful, Your Honour."

"Miss Tomkins," he barked. "How many times have you had sex with a married man?"

"I honestly don't know," she said. Amanda looked at her feet.

"You don't know," repeated Archie Morton. "Let me try to help you, Miss Tomkins. "Shall we agree more than ten times?"

"I can't remember. Possibly."

"Twenty times," said Archie.

"You are trying to show me in a way that is not me," said Sarah.

"I am trying to show you as a woman who enjoys casual sex," said Archie.

"No," shouted Sarah. "Never. The partners I chose are all..."

"Are all what?" asked the defence counsel.

Amanda remained seated.

"Ethan raped me," said Sarah.

"No, Miss Tomkins. That is not true. You consented to the events that took place by admitting you wanted sex, by rushing up the stairs, by leading the way with two men into the boardroom, by having intercourse with Ivan while Ethan watched, and then having sex with Ethan." He paused and turned to the jury. "That is what happened, isn't it, Miss Tomkins?" He didn't wait for an answer.

"Just one more question, Miss Tomkins. And this puzzles me. You have told this court that you willingly went up to the boardroom to have sex with Ivan Derbyshire. As you reached the room you realised that Edward Delaney was to be involved." He paused. "Why, Miss Tomkins, why did you not simply walk away and none of the subsequent events would have taken place?"

Amanda knew the answer to the question. Sarah was aroused and wanted sex with Ivan. "Say nothing," Amanda thought to herself.

"I wish I had," shouted Sarah.

"Had what, Miss Tomkins?" asked Archie.

"'Walked away', as you put it," she said.

"So, the members of the jury can base their decision

on your evidence that you were in that boardroom willingly?"

"I said 'No!'" shouted Sarah, defiantly.

Amanda decided to leave it at this point. She felt there would be no purpose served by re-examining the witness. She wanted the last thing ringing in the jurors' ears to be the word 'no'.

Not Guilty 8. Guilty 2. The law student considered not bothering to waste the bus fare again tomorrow as this case was all but over.

She returned to her flat alone and lonely. There were no messages from Ben and Trevor had not phoned her. The night hours seemed endless as she sat in court imagining the summary that Judge Clarke would deliver later the next morning. The two rapists would walk away laughing with their families and friends and go to the pub to celebrate their acquittal. Sarah would sneak away to a humiliating return to the reception desk at Heaton Van Sales, her reputation in tatters.

Her eyes were closing, and she was drifting. She simply had no further stamina left to review the four days of evidence. She found herself dreaming about being in the Sung Wong Toi Park in Kowloon and there was Fat FrEthan – both of them. They were each holding her hand. They sat down and FrEthan Wing Wey turned to her and smiled.

"Ben niao xian fei zao ru lin," he said.

A clumsy bird that flies first will get to the forest earlier.

She woke up and was immediately alert.

"What, Fat FrEthan. What is it? What am I missing?" she cried out.

She ran her hand through her hair and then she

remembered something. She leaped out of bed, catching her foot in the duvet. She hit the floor with a shudder. It only momentarily impeded her progress. She dashed to her desk where she opened her papers and searched for Monday's notes. She then re-read several police files. She was becoming animated as she sensed a lead. She turned over each page, skim-reading the contents, and then she went back to one particular section. She found the passage she was looking for and then she located the later testimony. She checked and re-checked. She went on to where Sarah had fallen. It was all there, and she had failed to realise its significance.

She rushed to the bathroom and threw cold water over her face.

"It's the hair. It's the colour of her bloody hair," she shouted out.

As his driver weaved his way through the Friday morning commuter traffic, Judge Maynard Clarke relaxed back into the cushioned rear seat of his judicial car and reflected on the readings which his monitor had recorded earlier in the morning. "147/85," he pondered. During a recent annual medical examination, his doctor had noted raised blood pressure. Before starting prescriptive treatment, he suggested that his patient, in order to eliminate 'white coat syndrome' (the stress of the doctor's surgery resulting in misleading results), buy a home monitor and record his BP each morning and again at the end of the day (but before the evening consumption of malt whisky).

His Honour knew that the systolic value (the reading showing the pressure as the blood leaves the heart through the arteries) was too high. He was pleased that the diastolic figure at '85', showing the pressure as the blood returns to the heart through the veins, was at a healthier level.

An hour later, in his room at the Nailton Crown Court, as he stared at Amanda Buckingham, had his blood pressure been taken, both readings would almost certainly have been considerably raised.

Archie Morton was frustrated and concerned. He had been caught completely off guard with the CPS's application to recall an earlier witness. Archie had tried to say 'no' but he had no idea what he was saying 'no' to or why he wanted to say 'no'. After a lot of multi-syllable verbosity his main reason for objecting was because the CPS had asked.

"I grant the application Miss Buckingham," declared Judge Clarke, "but be under no misapprehension: I can give you no latitude with your questions."

The CPS and Amanda had achieved the requisite permission from Judge Clarke, but it took several hours for the court officials and the police to locate the individual and bring him back to court.

At 11.59 on Friday morning of the trial of Ivan Derbyshire and Edward Delaney, the man stared out of the witness box looking bewildered and anxious. He confirmed his name and that he understood he was still under oath. He watched as Amanda Buckingham approached him.

"Mr Toskas," she said.

Despite all the events of the last five days, Judge Clarke secretly admired the prosecuting counsel. In his assessment, she had that special quality that marked her down as a barrister with a future.

"Mr Toskas," she repeated. "I want to revisit some of the evidence you gave to this court last Monday."

"I told the truth," he spluttered.

"Mr Toskas," she continued. "During the events of the Friday night party at Heaton Van Sales you told this court that you followed Ivan Derbyshire, Edward Delaney and Sarah Tomkins out of the staff canteen and up the stairs."

"I told the truth. Ivan told me to piss off and so I went back to the party."

"Yes. I am satisfied that you have correctly confirmed what you said."

"Your Honour," interrupted Archie Morton. "Where is this meaningless line of questions taking us?" he said.

"Sit down, Mr Morton," ruled the judge "Miss Buckingham. Please speed up your questioning."

"Thank you, Your Honour," said Amanda.

She looked down at her notes.

"Mr Toskas," she continued. "Did you tell this court that you returned to a particular girl."

Luca Toskas put his hands to his face.

"Yes," he said.

"What is her name?"

"Chaudra," he replied.

"And what colour hair does she have?" asked Amanda.

"Your Honour," angered Archie Morton, "this is a farce. We'll be told the name of her hairdresser if prosecuting counsel continues this approach."

"Miss Buckingham, I really can't permit your line of questioning much longer."

"Thank you, Your Honour," said Amanda.

She turned and faced the witness box.

"Mr Toskas. You have said that you returned to the party to be with a special girl. Yes or no?"

"Yes, Chaudra. She's dark-haired," he answered. "She is beautiful."

"Can I confirm that, please Mr Toskas? Chaudra is dark-haired. A brunette."

"Yes," said the witness.

"Yes," repeated the prosecution counsel. "That is what you said to the police officer who interviewed you on the evening of the party. He specifically recorded her name and that she was dark-skinned and a brunette." Amanda paused.

"So why did you tell this court that she was blonde?"

Luca reddened in his face. He looked down and started to fidget.

"I don't remember," he spluttered. "Chaudra is dark. She is what I told you. I can't have said that."

"Shall I have the recording of your evidence given last Monday played back to the members of the jury?" asked Amanda.

"P-perhaps I said she was blonde," muttered an increasingly desperate Luca.

But the wheels were coming off. He tried to argue that he could not tell the difference between the two colours, that Chaudra often changed the colour of her hair and that he had been confused.

Finally, Amanda pounced.

"Mr Toskas. I put it to you that, in fact, you did not go down the stairs, but you waited and, after a few moments in time, you went up the stairs?"

Tears filled his eyes.

"Please. I'm so sorry. I'm going to church every day to ask for forgiveness. I am so sorry".

"Why are you so sorry?" asked Amanda. "Why, Mr Toskas?" she repeated.

He looked across the court room towards the two defendants.

"I can't tell you. Ethan will beat me up," he said.

She now took the terrified witness, step by step, thought the events of the Friday evening. He had waited for several minutes before following the three participants up the stairs. He said that he wanted to know what happened. When he reached the third floor the door was closed but the window blind had not been fully lowered. He had watched the events with a clear view. He said he could see and hear everything.

When Ethan had left the room, he had hidden along the corridor and then, moments later, watched Ivan leave. He looked into the room and saw that Sarah was sitting in a chair. He went down the stairs and then heard her open the door. As he turned around and looked up the stairs, he found her collapsing into his arms. He said that there was blood on her hand.

"Mr Toskas," said Amanda. "I want you please to think carefully about my next question. When Sarah was struggling on the table, and being held down, did you hear her say anything?"

"She was fighting to get free. Ivan was holding her down."

"Did she say anything?" asked Amanda.

"She shouted out "No!"," said the witness.

"Are you sure? Could she have said 'oh'?" asked Amanda.

"No. She said "No" and then Ethan hit her. He and Ivan were like animals. She was in terrible trouble."

Ethan leaped up and threw himself at the protection screen that guarded the defendants from the open courtroom.

"Luca. You're a fucking dead man walking," he bellowed. Amanda stood in horror as the real Edward Delaney presented himself to the world. He looked deranged. His eyes bulged; the veins in his neck looked like they were trying to force their way out of his skin. Several of the jury recoiled.

Ethan thumped the screen and spittle dripped down like rain on a windscreen.

Eventually he was restrained by the court officials. When sense returned, he slumped down into seat with the heaviness of a man who knows he's in serious trouble.

After that, events moved quickly. The defendants changed their plea and admitted to the offences with which they were charged in order to try and mitigate their custodial sentences.

Their families and friends emptied from the visitor's gallery and never returned.

The law student sat, open mouthed, his eyes flitting back and forth in disbelief at what he had just witnessed. He never updated his tally score. He was glad he had made a late decision to return to the courtroom.

Judge Clarke thanked and dismissed the jury, remanded the prisoners in custody and deferred sentencing until two weeks' time. He warned Ivan Derbyshire and Edward Delaney that they faced custodial sentences.

As the court rose, Amanda caught the eye of the Judge. There was hardly a flicker of recognition but there was, perhaps, an imperceptible nod of his head. Archie Morton refused to acknowledge his peer and stormed out of the building.

Amanda later spoke to her Chambers. She was told that there was a bundle of papers being couriered to her home detailing a case of death by dangerous driving starting at the magistrate's court on Monday morning. To her relief she was defending the motorist. As she headed for her car she checked again and felt disappointed that there was no message about her cat.

There was, however, a text from Sarah Tomkins asking if they could meet. Reluctantly, Amanda decided to agree. She felt that the receptionist had been through so much over the last few weeks. It was an ill-advised move, but she said she would see her in the park later in the afternoon. She knew that the fresh air would do her good in the light of another text message she had received:

'Well done AB. Sorry, but u're not my type. Let's move on. THH.'

She spoke just one word: "Diu."

As they later came together in the open spaces Amanda felt a sense of admiration for her.

"Thank you for agreeing to meet with me," said Sarah. "I'm a bit tearful but at least it's all over."

"Briefly, Sarah," said Amanda "and then you must never contact me again."

They walked together along a tree-lined path. They watched as two dogs chased each other.

"Did you hear that Debbie Derbyshire lost her baby last night?" she asked.

Amanda said nothing. She allowed a period of silence to continue.

"You know I can't find the words," said Sarah.

"I did my job," said Amanda.

"I wanted to tell you my news," said Sarah. She ignored the silence. "I'm going to train as a social worker. When I nursed my Gran last year, I found something I wanted to do. I'm going to study to be a manager of a care home."

"Sounds good," said Amanda. "The cut in pay will hurt."

"I have all the money I need, I'm to receive a decent pay-off,"" said Sarah. "Mr Heaton, the chairman, phoned me from his holiday home." He had listened carefully to the advice given to him by Yvette, the personnel director.

Amanda paused. She wanted to know something.

"Sarah, what will happen to Luca?" she asked.

"Unbelievable. The lads from the office collected him and took him back to the depot. He was kissed by all the girls." She paused. "A particular brunette took charge of him."

"Chaudra," said Amanda.

Sarah laughed.

"Justice has won the day. Isn't that right, Amanda?" Before the barrister could reply, she went on, "Did you know that a clerk from accounts has gone to the police? She's claiming she was also raped by Ivan and Ethan."

Amanda winced. She took Sarah's left hand and squeezed it.

They shared a fond, almost sisterly, embrace and, as Sarah walked away, Amanda watched her go.

As she turned towards the Tube station her phone vibrated. She looked down at the message:

'He's better. He's has had small meal. One more night to be sure. Collect him tomorrow mid-morning. B.'

She stood still, beaming, and then skipped down the

stairs into the underground station. As she neared her Clerkenwell flat there was a further text message from Ben.

Ivan Derbyshire and Edward Delaney were sentenced to five and seven years in prison. Ethan took to the brutal regime like a duck to water and began to make several questionable associates. Ivan became reclusive and needed medical help for depression. He was not helped by the disappearance of Debbie who, once she had been discharged from hospital following the loss of her baby, relocated to the Lake District with her son. She found work in a Windermere restaurant and, within a year, she had begun a new relationship and became pregnant. She never saw Ivan again.

During the investigation at Heaton Van Sales, the police uncovered a discrepancy in the sales invoice for the van transaction, which had triggered the party. It was later revealed that the money due to be paid was being collected by a Guernsey-based associated company and HMRC tax inspectors were undertaking a comprehensive audit and review. Not long after, the chairman was back in the country facing prosecution for VAT-related fraud. The business subsequently went into liquidation and was bought out by a competitor. The girls on reception all survived but, by now, Luca had left. He and Chaudra emigrated to Italy to begin a new life together.

Sarah Tomkins decided to fly to Portugal for a week in the sun. She was soon talking to the man sitting in the window seat and they arrived at Faro in a decidedly relaxed manner. He was into property sales and Sarah accepted his invitation for her to visit him at his villa. After a repeat trip several weeks later, this became a more permanent arrangement. She remained in close contact with her mother and tried to persuade her to join her and her new partner in the Iberian sunshine.

Archie Morton reacted petulantly to the loss of the case but quickly recovered and was soon back in court. Judge Maynard Clarke overcame his blood pressure problems by adopting a vegetarian diet and losing two stone in weight.

Early on the Saturday morning following the end of the trial, Zach put Amanda through her paces in the boxing ring and insisted she swam forty lengths of the pool. She feasted on bowls of fresh fruit and figs. She returned home and decided to wear her hair loose, a white shirt and jeans.

She arrived at the vets late in the morning. Ben brought Rumpole out to her in his cage. He immediately tried to lick her fingers which she had pushed through the wire cover.

She turned to the vet.

"I received your text message," she said.

Ben looked at her.

"You've a spare ticket for the theatre, tonight," she laughed.

Ben said nothing.

"I think I can consent to that," she smiled.

As she put her cat in the back of her car, she realised that she had no idea what they were going to see.

THE END

AMANDA BUCKINGHAM: AN EARLY HISTORY

Amanda was born on 3 June 1983 on Kowloon Island, Hong Kong. She was an only child and registered as being British. Her father, Arthur Grosvenor Marin Buckingham, was deputy head of the civil service in the Territory. He played a pivotal role in negotiating the handover from Britain to China.

These were turbulent times, with anti-British riots and bombings which were encouraged by the Chinese authorities. There was an influx of Vietnamese refugees of whom, by 1988, there were 50,000 on the island. There were continuing fears that the Chinese would abandon their commitment to their 'one country, two systems' pledge. The transfer of sovereignty eventually took place in 1997 when Amanda was fourteen years old.

Her early years were dominated by her father's descent into heavy drinking and libidinous behaviour. She was the product of a brief dalliance with a hotel receptionist, Julie Neo, a Hong Kong citizen. Her father died the day after the transfer of Hong Kong to China by the British government.

Amanda was educated at the Diocesan School for Girls in Hong Kong learning Cantonese and later French much to the annoyance of her father. After his death it was decided, in conjunction with the British authorities, that Amanda should move to London.

She arrived with a dual passport and a trust fund of several million pounds. Her uncle, and a firm of London solicitors, were the trustees. She knew that she would be eligible for half the money when she reached twenty-one years of age and the balance when she was thirty.

She took her time and spent the early days with her aunt, Eileen and her stepbrother, Jonathan, who both amused and irritated her in equal measure. Her uncle was rarely at home.

Her academic record, including twelve GCSE's and four A-Levels including Law, resulted in her achieving entrance to Lady Margaret Hall, Oxford, including a year at Pantheon-Assas, in Paris. In 2005, she graduated with a First Class, Oxon in Law (Jurisprudence). She included European Constitutional Law in her areas of expertise.

After coming down from Oxford University Amanda sailed through the Bar Vocational Course. A pupillage was secured for her at Hartington Chambers, a leading London criminal law set, Amanda was called to the Bar in 2007.

We first meet Amanda in the second novella forming a series of titles inspired by iconic cinema classics (*Novella Nostalgia* series). In *Twelve Troubled Jurors* she is the defence barrister and is mentioned briefly as most of the action takes place in the jury room.

ABOUT THE AUTHOR

After spending over a decade as a lawyer Oliver runs a dispute resolution consultancy that helps businesses resolve their commercial disputes through dialogue and negotiation. He is Chairman of Bedfordshire's region of Wooden Spoon, a charity that helps socially, mentally, and physically disadvantaged children and he is also a volunteer at a local homeless outreach organisation. He lives in Bedford with his wife and daughter.

Oliver published his first novella, Gloriana, which was

inspired by the Tom Cruise film, *Valkyrie*, in September 2018. Using the background of 'Brexit', *Gloriana* is a thunderous political thriller with an unexpected twist in the tale and it has received critical acclaim including being "highly commended" in the 2020 London Page Turner Awards.

In 2019 *The Courageous Witness* launched the career of mesmeric barrister Amanda Buckingham and the BriefCase Series and *The Star Witness* is Case 2 of Season 1. There is much more to come from Amanda in Case 3 Season 1!

Contact Oliver:

Instagram	@oliverrichbell
Facebook	oliverjamesrichbell
Twitter	@richbelloliver